HORSE RIDING IN *EAST* SUSSEX

HORSE RIDING IN *EAST* SUSSEX
(A Moral Tale)

By

Jon Capin

Hamilton & Co. Publishers Ltd
London

© Copyright 1999
Jon Capin

The right of Jon Capin
to be identified as author of this work
has been asserted by him in accordance with
Copyright, Designs and Patents Act 1988

All rights reserved.
No reproduction, copy or transmission of this
publication may be made without written permission.
No paragraph of this publication may be reproduced,
copied or transmitted
save with the written permission or in accordance
with the provisions of the Copyright Act 1956 (as
amended).
Any person who does any unauthorised act
in relation to this publication may be liable
to criminal prosecution and civil
claims for damage.

All characters in this publication are fictitious and any
resemblance to real persons, living or dead, is purely
coincidental.

Paperback ISBN 1 901668 92 4

Publisher

Hamilton & Co. Publishers Ltd
10 Stratton Street
Mayfair
London

Soundtrack recordings:
Extracts from albums -
Lick My Decals Off, Baby
Shiny Beast
Trout Mask Replica
Strictly Personal

All titles © Captain Beefheart and his Magic Band

From forty on
You learn from the sharp cuts and jags
Of poems that have come to pieces
In your crude hands how to assemble
With more skill the arbitrary parts
Of ode or sonnet, while time fosters
A new impulse to conceal your wounds
From her and from a bold public,
Given to pry.

R.S.Thomas

The wind blew low, the wind blew high;
the stakes were low, the stakes were high.

Don Van Vliet

CHAPTER ONE

From his ponderous position on the cultivated green, municipally captioned 'West Hill', even he could almost believe that a distant faint cloud hugging the seaward horizon was both near and far, another European Community Fatherland of post impressionist art, fine wine, garlic, haute couture, philosophy, Jean Luc Godard, *Je t'aime,* Jeanne Moreau and Jean Marie le Pen.

Newcomers and holidaymakers noticing skyline stratocumulus usually claim they can see France from this spot while locals preach their geological truths of empiricism and cartography.

Wry folks the natives, you see. Modest, but wry.

The 'East Hill', to give the neighbouring, stunted jetty of a cliff plateau prosaic admission of common identity, lay to the left a quarter mile away, sea fretted out of focus while slightly higher, with the Old Town nestling between the two dominating heights, defensively cupped lower and randomly occupied by a celebrated prolifery of high rated alehouses.

Turning his heavily creased, sweaty, ex-Luftwaffian, fading black leather trench coat-collar up to the cold and precociously damp, insouciant, westerly wind, to resemble a once chart-topping, successful, ageing rock star who now survives on the cabaret circuit, he forced his penetrating gaze towards the small excited crowd surrounding the newly discovered corpse. The act struggled to curtail his compelling view of the colludingly quaint, coomb created Old Town down below amidst the two lofty, book-ended landmarks of lauded tourism.

A secure and comforting dipsomaniac paradise forever standing brash, breezy and balmy down the eastern slope of his current position that he knew and loved so well.

And so often.

> A heaven therein
> to drink shants of sin
> wherein
> he'd rather be.
> Loving to drink,
> to drink lovingly of life,
> enamoured to some neighbour
> or lover or thief or wife,
> closer than free;
> or hangman's psychotic cousin
> he could deign to handle or not.
> There is always another bar
> in this wonderland
> of illusion and dependence to adopt.

But he hated this. Especially this type of repulsive familiar crime.

His world was guilty again. Every man was guilty again.

The planet, the galaxy was guilty again.

Some surprise.

It never stops.

"So who introduced beatific, smouldering, conceptual gems like money, and religion, and territory? To confound and enchant the brashest and trashiest of egos in their brave new flat world?" he wondered. "And added possessive pronouns as a pernicious tease? What a doltish, dirlish brew! Always to be problems. Always.

And this sudden deed involves one or more of the trinity. I'm already sure."

Beyond this publicly owned sudden police presencing grass tableland, obsessively husbanded by paid local authority degraders dreaming their lottery lives, his vision, again persistently seeking brief redemption away from the imminent disquiet, chose to condescendingly view the foreshortened, westward stretch of Albion coast.

So beyond Newtown, advertising at the base of West Hill, he scanned over the versatile waterside of defiance, elasticity and indecision that geologically concluded observation at the sharp bluff, Holywell pre Beachy Head. Scarcely perceived in the morning light through local haze veiling its long celebrated tourist beauty all under a continuum of high, relentless, rain-laden, billowing cloud as if forever looping on a victorious, Victorian, magic lantern show.

When and if he deigned this littoral spectacle as aesthetic postcard print through camera obscura deemed not. As today was not Art appreciation day.

No. No. No.

But playful thoughts of submerged, eternal passions clouded his recently crowded mind as he continued gazing out from the headland in harnessed trepidation over the disturbed dominion of swelling implacability. On he mused.

The sumptuous sea plays sweet violence with the dissolved and vanquished ingredient salt.

Afflatus on high.

The sole drowned brethren and silent lover
in turbid vicissitudes
a token togetherness equal in a sometime.

He wanted something high. Higher or lower than this.

The job, that is.

The job with the pension while they are still being proffered.

The job carrying the recognised legality of all and everything.

From his distracted distance the body seemed to causally demonstrate an exaggerated attitude of consumed loss. In time. If left. A depravity.

To loudly advertise nutritious, high protein, seagull snacks.

The parsimonious sun demonstrated a lesson of inadvergency entertaining in spectrumed snatches stolen through sullen, early morning, low cumulus, as if remembering the etiquette of the situation. Somewhere in the cloud-scape a Boeing 747, the interior tentatively unrealistic, the exterior fraught with gravity, sustaining its glidepath into Gatwick, is occasionally glimpsed from below. Shrugging his shoulders and turning to face the day's problem, Detective Inspector Fulke Swettervil thought, "The sooner the better to imbibe later," as he pushed through the blueness of cloth and politics to arrive over the victim. To quantify; the dead was male, young, long haired, clothed in the colours of darkness and beautifully broken; and until very recently attractive to a solicitous some.

These concerned ones he clarified inside as general suspects, *it is often someone the victim knows*, post structuralist in action they told themselves, post modern in clothes posing to others, fragile babies in black they seemed to him.

"Why does the human body always appear beautiful in some different aesthetic equation when distorted or mangled, moments before the rush of realisation and revulsion overtake thought?" he pondered, while noticing children ape Himalayan climbers on the craggy stepped slopes of the truncated hillock, overlooking ocean, where the castle and men breathed a privileged freedom until long term crumbling began to permanently ruin.

But bodies are not to be left in holiday areas, the spaces where happy families enter, his reasoning played. This particular one meant a bent that others may not realise and would bias against the self evident ruling. Try telling that to the hung council. They would need to employ a cadaver warden next to run parallel with the canine equivalent. To get there quicker and tidier than the police. They could...if anyone could...persuade the potential corpse to ring in just before...

"More work to do now. Who found it?" He wondered aloud, looking round for the obvious clues in faces and hierarchical positions that should point to that specific uniform of successful diligence, instead of simply asking for his or her whereabouts as he walked towards the tense knot of dark blue and flashing light, blue and yellow humanity semi-surrounded by vehicled whiteness with buzzed rap-like radio messages momentarily filling the ears only to sharply disappear again into contrasted silence.

The morning's mood now resolutely established, it satisfied him to smugness sensing that others of the team quickly realised and adapted to fit as if their material wealth depended on this. He knew and was filled with a mixture of pride, confusion and assimilation when he often heard jocular mumblings from the ranks commenting on the appropriateness of his name for the job.

His immigrant parent chose well.

The precursory morning was passing quietly on its usual terms.

Contradicting as it did so on both the English coastal weather's indecisive and gambled rate of change from cold to warmer moist air, and the noticeably excited, busying crowd of humanity's random stuttered to staggered to minion clustered movements around their recent morbid, touched by human hand, discovery.

Advection fog was quickly making visibility no concern or consequence. People seemed to mock it, with mime, in their slow motioned, indecisive and retreading movements like a march of decaying, death dolls in a cheap horror film on a furtive youngster's video screen.

CHAPTER TWO

D.I. Fulke Swettervil pushed through the pondering masses to the young patrolman who discovered the victim, who is now dreaming of promotion, money, women and the liberty of a coastal cottage in Wales for his retirement, but realises the necessity to find more lifeless bodies to ensure this future and decides he will probably begin looking later today. After lunch.

Speech abruptly came between them.

With little volume but a meaning monochromity.

Utterances in a Sussex tinge.

"You?" The detective inspector, softly surprised on recognition.

"Yes, sir."

"So?" Impatience prompting etiquette.

"Er...Morning, sir?"

"Well?"

P.C. Pile looked unsure.

"Tell!" The described low volume wavered to slight.

P.C. Pile wondered if D.I. Swettervil's louder imperative was a feigned pose.

"Oh, murder, sir...sorry, sir...definitely, sir." P.C. Pile understood to answer and articulated so.

An action of nerve caused itch somewhere high on D.I. Swettervil's still straight spined shape.

Elbow to hand movement he scratched the side of his head.

"Sure. Not sunbathing then?"

"Definite, sir."

"How the quietus?"

The nerve moved over. He did too and scratched the other side.

"Quie?...er...We don't know exactly yet, sir...But something blunt."

"Quite." Over the shoulder of the young policeman at an approved distance he could see an old man videoing the misted seascape.

"Sorry, sir?"

"Oh, nothing...You were saying?"

"Would you like to…?"

"No, I would not! I'd get in the way of the photographer...When did it happen?"

"Not long. Few hours. Rigor mortis has begun, though."

"Mmmm!...mm…Anybody recognise him?"

"We don't...You might...sir?"

"I will wait...for your report."

The nerve stabilised. He did too and scratched the back of his head.

"We're looking for anything. Some clothing still unaccounted for."

"Keep looking for anything then."

"Yes, sir."

Scratched close tiny tidy hair on nape of neck.

The patrolman had discovered quickly, as had the world, that this signified their leader was in deep thought, hence concentrating hard on the morning's new events.

"I'll view...everything at the...mortuary. You're in charge here."

"Am I? I am. Yes sir. Thank you sir."

> Though exactly
> what he was
> going to do
> Police Constable Pile
> had not
> the wraith
> of a clue.

Both noticed the ambulance crew loading the red blanketed body to commence its post mortem route, and the Park Ranger van simultaneously driven close to take what would be the next imagined parking space. Both noticed the embossed gold lettered HPR capped form stumbling headfirst out of the vehicle to jerkily recover his dark blue uniformed balance causing reference books of wild flowers, rare insects, seabirds, mushrooms, toadstools and hallucinogenics and their antidotes to chaotically follow him onto the grass to his wide eyed burbling embarrassment.

"The encyclopaedia of all knowledge there needs to talk, Pile. See if he's got anything to say," mentioned the Detective Inspector to the Constable, as the former slumped away towards the road with a brief wave of acknowledgement to the emergency vehicle driver now on the road and accelerating away from the group.

No-one bothers to watch or comment on a passing ambulance unless it concerns them or theirs.

The detective knew the next time this concluded transferred shell met his presence would be on his next periodical musing of the same in the town's charnel house of non-remitting variety.

P.C. Pile patiently waited for the Park Ranger to steady body, thoughts and reference book collection before forming speech. D.I. Swettervil was still scratching itchy stubble on his lower neck hence delving deeper into thoughts of the morning's discovery when he almost crashed into a rotund, ankle-less, shiny shell-suited, smiling, nuclear family of four, on their manic, holiday, pre-noon, tunnel vision scurry for bland colour injected, fizzy, sugar water in a brashly printed can, hoodwinked totally like millions of other thought controlled urbanites by evangelically zealous, imperialist, multi-national conmen on a relentless global advertise and conquer spree. His vague, mumbled, confused curse-cum-apology was not picked up by the tightly gathered, thirsty troupe as distance speedily increased between the momentarily, near missed, scuttling protagonists.

After unrewarding dialogue with the nature trail maker P.C. Pile stood waiting in case of reformation. This state was not unusual. He knew.

D.I. Swettervil forced another 'Fisherman's Friend' into his mouth. He knew he needed the velvet syrupy taste of their solid, unswerving, unique punch now as his ageing, rusting, poor man's Aston Martin stunk so highly and religiously of functional fuel that this learned appetite of provincial obliquity quickly became habit pleasing, an awareness somewhere near vanity. The result was that he no longer tasted the petrol vapours as the lozenge dominated most relevant senses. Many mechanics tried to seek for his leak but none not the one found anything of it.

He merely renamed his two doored, four seated transport Treblinka and smoothed four gears forward or intentionally jerked one to reverse without so much as a goy's curse to rapidly become movement automatic.

As he inclined towards the road running alongside the West Hill to reclaim his exclusive, polluting transport, the edge of his sight noticed to turn full and labour on two, waving, young girls riding small, Welsh Mountain ponies clearly exhibiting Houyhnhnm grace and Stubbian analytical beauty about to commence disappearing below the rear of East Hill towards Fairlight, the next pretty, rich and scenic village along the coast. For several seconds he gazed into a hazy swimming recollection of his own, now teenage daughter, Jackie and her Swiftian love of these beasts; if he only knew where his paltry, paltered, ex-Perfidia Pansy had taken her. His ex-mate for life must have had taste at one time, he thought, and smiled as he scuffed his thick, vegetarian soled, industrial shock absorption, *German named* fashion boots in the dampened ground flattening deathcaps, common earth balls, monk hoods and dehydrating dog turds on the calculated route to his decaying, intoxicating conveyance.

It was such a superlatively fertile summer. For everything, in the garden and the countryside.

All the biologists and meteorologists commented on it. Some even celebrated. Too well.

An already heat stupor-suffering common wasp - *vespula vulgaris* - sheltering in the car's leather shade on the wrong pennate of fate, suffocated instantly when Fulke took off and carefreely threw the heavy, black leather, maternal heirloom bequeathed to him on her death onto the worn, biscuit coloured hide passenger seat. The coat fell displaying the name Schweibb-Ervil labourly labelled in colour on the collar (*his mother insisted on hyphenating the new name making it seem more credibly English. She stubbornly claimed it suggested poise. An English aristocratic characteristic she insisted, as mothers often do*). Followed by his tall, square shouldered presence promptly filling the driver's space under an aura of thoughtful urgency that clouded his countenance.

Treblinka trembled with vibration. Fulke Swettervil's sweaty, long, straining fingers vainly patted his hair as he looked into the amalgam failing, rear view mirror, fastened his distressed seat-belt and pushed in the Captain's cassette.

Gimme dat harp boy sang out. Tainting all tranquillity. Four speaker proud.

Headlights displayed and highway code regulatory use of the back vision glass, his beloved, ageing, metallic blue, two litre, four cylinder, Ford Capri with rostyle wheels noisily drove off into the low cloud. Seemingly becoming distantly incorporeal.

CHAPTER THREE

Sylvia sat, white plastic chaired, outside 'The Mermaid' cafe on the Old Town sea-front gazing forlornly ahead. Looking towards, but disregarding, the beach scene of lined but cluttered clinker fishing boats, small rowing craft, dirty plastic drums, and neat and discarded tar-stained tackle peeked at between the fleet of beano buses and container lorries parked near to the tall, thin, darkly painted, looming, redundant net huts. She did not hear the cries of the squabs and their flying sentinels feathered for survival as her mind was far too busy wondering whether or not she should write to her mother in the Western Colonies informing her of the splendid, new shoes she had purchased in London. This high heeled, fashionable footwear was urgently needed to decorate her ravishing, languorous, new dress, blue inside and out, absolutely guaranteed to excite every sex everywhere, she would no doubt communicate clearly to her parent. Or, with the slight smell of fresh paint still hanging over catering establishment and nostril, should she just write a new poem about the refurbishment of 'The Mermaid' as a metaphor for life without a brown shirted father in any post war Macedonian bee keeping group?

The poem would take less time, she mused, watching two young women in patched skirts and woolly holed cardigans with dirty, long braided hair determinedly handing out photographs and booklets of propaganda that claimed horrific animal experiments went on in British laboratories to anyone wishing a quiet life.

Sylvia wondered why each wore a lapel badge showing a white crow on a black background. The now twice named eatery she frequented stood between a fish restaurant and a fish shop and cooked this named vertebrate more tastefully, more sensually, more vivaciously superior than all other South Coast eateries of this bemused isle as acclaimed in various world and national newspaper restaurant articles. Folks travelled for miles and miles and miles just to eat here, sometimes crossing national borders, never to return.

The restaurant's new, interior image of dried local flowers, tasteful Yorkshire stone wall and art deco mermaid lamps had been slowly accepted by the usual seafaring clientele; some even noticed, and this was easy seduction to the hungry travellers who over-volubly expressed their delight at the change.

Would it work though all though?

Would it matter, many articulated?

The world's largest and cheapest bag of chips sized bap butties dispensed inside to individual taste, carry their own publicity and destiny.

The radio was loudly playing **Kandy Korn** but nobody desired or ached that way.

All stayed savoury.

Tables and chairs outside showed the place was open and running.

Access occurred around dawn, and sold breakfasts to the sober or mere cups of tea to the hungover, courageous kinship of mortals who go to sea, flying the British and Canadian flags, to vie, along with many other, close unwelcome and uninvited European nation boats, for the same, cold blooded, aquatic prizes.

Sylvia was the only customer at her table on which stood her several, now empty, see through glass cups of coffee, *naturally reserved for special customers*, resting in lesser defraction, sat in their visually uninterrupted saucers along with her supermarket bought, marble effect notebook, some of the thesaurus trained pages showing spilled evidence of her liquid choice. She slowly began to notice that consolidated caffeine spots had also splashed onto her figure hugging, blue velvet jeans, her white deck shoes and table leaning, cream canvas bag, containing the obligatory, plastic wrap raincoat along with recent metaphysical rhymes by the newly recommended, South Coast writers, but fortunately missed her off white, angora, tunic sweater.

Her sigh of realisation held a mixture of exasperation and gratitude quickly turning to surprise as she became aware and took instant advantage of the heat of the sun abruptly pushed through the cloud cover, by pushing her dyed blonde head back to monopolise the rays.

Heard inside the café, a monotonous, middle aged, chain smoking female voice complains loudly of butter spread on white bread that should have carried vegetable spread margarine. Followed by an establishment incredulous sigh insidiously proclaiming, can we ever be right?

Another two tight blue permed, past peaked women leave the building and walk slowly but determinedly. One matter of factly grating to the other, "He'll be in the soddin' pub."

"Which one?"

"The nearest bugger to 'ere. The one we just passed. He'll be pissed if we don't find 'im."

"Oh!"

"There it is!" They stop to decide.

"You can go back if you want and save our seats while I go in and drag 'im out."

"You know he'll be in there?"

"I bloody know!"

"You won't stay in then?"

"You must be bloody joking, Moira! That'll be the day! I'll drag the bugger out. So I will."

"All right. See you back here?"

"You certainly will!"

"It's a day out for all of us, not just a bloody pissup for 'im. It's always the bloody same. The selfish bugger." To herself and/or her departing friend.

Two tables away a middle aged, pencil thin moustached man, with a considerable paunch of uncomfortable, subcultured dissatisfaction, sat eating a fried egg sandwich smothered with brown sauce, trying unsuccessfully to quickly lick enough yellow of the egg and brown of the relish dripping down his chin before it stains his unprotected, navy blue blazer while staring at two pigeons on next door's guttering exhibiting excesses of dalliance. Albert E. Burst felt this last day blues like a haunting. Tomorrow he had to leave and go back home to North London. To the abattoir. To work. Still at least he had seen a celebrity, he could tell his mates. I wonder what she's famous for though, he wondered, with her good looks and the expensive clothes she wears she must be a well known film star or something.

The clouds hung lower and greyer advertising showers of inconvenience. Sylvia knew there was no need to worry at this present showing, being so used to her adopted country's weather, as it would very possibly turn into a wonderful sunny day. Though, she would often admit, on first arriving in this cosy, cute, little realm she assumed the weather, her passion felt through first on a particular day, was the only weather to be experienced until the corresponding night.

"Allroight Miss Plarth?" A clean-shaven fisherman rushing by warmly speaks and smiles, looking the poetess up and down, admiring her always trim, desirable frame.

"Oh hello," Sylvia replies warmly.

"Carn't stop. Wu're a little bit spaced, as they say, so we're orff to sea." His designer stubbled companion calls back, slyly giggling, carrying the same appreciative thoughts in mind.

"We all are in some indefinable way boys," she murmured quietly knowing they would not hear.

"The only place to be!" said the first one grinning.

"See yar!" alternated both as they smiled admitting to each other their instant gratification choice of the moment.

"We'll be barck to see you around tonoight, Slyv'!" the least polite of the two fishermen called back.

Their voices starting to fade.

She remembered them with others of their warmth.

Not so long back when cruising through Newtown, correctly in her United States of American way, she allowed a waiting car out of a side-street to go ahead of her vehicle. The ungrateful auto immediately sped, exhaust gases blowing noisily, a little further up the road to slow and dawdle dangerously close to the polished chrome, waxed body, classic red sports car she was driving. Its tight-cropped-haired occupants began to shout crude, suggestive remarks at her beauty and her sex, confident of little or no comeback until their rusted conveyance presently stopped and a small crowd of indigenous "patriots" quickly left to commence moving towards her self, sat now transfixed with a mixture of disbelief and dread in the consummate car behind. Dire straited in her sitting duck posture she could only watch when a propitious, ghetto blasting van loaded with these Old Town "beachboys" passing by, stopped, sympathised with her plight and quickly readdressed the situation with noise, fisticuffs, discord and pitilessness.

Cold shivers ran through her prodigiously sensitive frame at this recollection.

She would eternally be grateful.

Maybe I should go to sea with them. Re-emerged present thoughts. Since that day I have been invited out several times. It could be what my work needs. I have never really worked that seadog imagery. She tensed her pen now, ready to begin her letter home.

She had made her decision.

Mother would receive the benefit.

CHAPTER FOUR

The waitress appeared bringing the middle aged man's pudding of rhubarb crumble and thick steaming custard. He watched with fear lining his three chinned, blue nosed face as she almost stumbled spilling his hot, lumpy desire, to just as quickly recover showing a triumphant, white-toothed smile that dazzled the morning. She carefully placed the dish on his table and for a few seconds watched him eat.

Which was swiftly with the relish of the failed entrepreneur instinctively knowing his last chance disappeared a long time before.

Her satisfied smile was leaving her lips as she began to speak politely to Sylvia.

"Can oi' ged you anyfin' 'lse, missus?" Having listened to all the gossip and realised the importance of this beautiful, literary, sometime blonde icon.

"Oh thank you. That is so kind of you to ask. Let me see. Could you get me a lettuce, tomato and cress with mayonnaise on brown please if that's no trouble? Oh, and with lots of sliced mushroom. Is that possible?"

"Yers, missus'" Still successfully tongue-damping her bubble gum.

"Oh, and another cup of your pleasant coffee, if that's OK, too?'"

"Yers, missus. Roight away." The girl smiled brightly now, wishing she had not enquired and wondering when this celebrity will stop talking.

Sylvia glimpsed at her wristwatch and wondered about the time of the carnival that night. Whether the weather would improve and shall she see her two friends, Malcolm and Fulke in 'The Duke of Wellington' afterwards. She mused as to why the waitress wore a T shirt showing a white crow cupped in caring hands.

She propped her pen and commenced carefree, cultured calligraphy without so much as a deep breath.

Dear Dear Mother,

So good to read your letter, though not sure when and from where it was sent, but it must still be the English Western Colonies. Hah Hah!! Soon to be called the Spanish Colonies by default!! Only joking, mother. It's quite a common joke over here how the English language will lose out to the Spanish. Many a word hey?

You have not moved again, Mother, have you, surely? I know I lost the children but really you always pick up the people and things I misplace, do you not? May you continue to do so.

I shopped only last week at that famous London department store named Harrods. You must have heard of the place? I ensured that anything of value or importance I would buy from there rather than anywhere else in the city even though the price may be higher as it surely must be the most prestigious shopping mall in England and ...the bonus!...you can show off for weeks merely by carrying their plastic name bag around. And that's me Mother, isn't it?!

I did buy my new blue shoes in their boutique area but not my new dress. I was very lucky there. That came instead from a local hippie shop as they call them here run by all ages of cigarette smelling, autumn flower frocked feminists with long flat dark hair sometimes greying, brown teeth, skin decorated with an amalgam of baroque tattoos and wearing rings through one or the other nostril. Sometimes both. To find anything in one of these 1970's places you have to stumble your way through bead curtaining, smelly hanging carpets and metal ringing mobiles, while at the same time avoiding the strong unpleasant smelling smoke emitting from joss sticks strategically set to suffocate you. Yes! They still burn those horrible smelling things here. Mostly when I am around it seems, and I thought the Brits had more sense than the Americans.

Anyway Mother, I feel young again. Wearing these garments I feel so chic. I could easily seduce the whole trivia of restrained English maledom all along this South Coast.

My postmark will show you where I have settled. I feel like I never want to move again. It is a lovely little hideaway on the English Costa del Sol and I have some wonderful friends here, mostly male. No surprises there, Mother! One is a successful author with a cult following, I always thought that was the nicest following to have. His name is on the book you will find enclosed, along with his picture. And the other is a sweet policeman with a strong literary bent who writes, as I do, poems and stories. Here is one of his primitive and stark, but tragic and too beautiful works.

    SNOWFALL
    Sharon is a slut
    has been painted
    in yellow gloss
    large and neat,
    on the tarmac slope
    beneath vain feet,
    but lays hidden
    under thick snow
    still falling
    on the envious
    and the proud.
    This will be something
    positively uplifting
    to read,
    through dark shades,
    when the sun
    fights off

this enemy of heat.

He has a smouldering darkness delicately hidden inside his warm personality which I find very attractive. This pulsates occasionally, surfacing in his face and underlying in his work.

I think possibly you will understand this too.

This pretty southern backwater I have chosen to settle in has some charming idiosyncrasies, Mother. For instance, the town claims to encourage business into its centre, but blocks off some of its roads for weeks. It claims to encourage tourism, but roadworks appear during the whole summertime every year. There was a pretty town centre cricket field situated here, unique to any town anywhere in the world you would think, that was soon smothered with a shopping centre looking like any other shopping centre in any other town in the country. Mother, you now know that cricket is an important game they play here, like baseball, remember, and that shopping centre? Well, the locals now call it "the prison" as they say it has many small windows on the outside giving that particular look. The genuine King of Ireland lives and drinks here, too, and they even seem to be rewriting the history books by repositioning the 1066 Norman landings further along the coast, nearer to this town, to offset the building of a freeway.

Such dizzy fun mother! Such euphoria!

And the real biggie, Mother! One you will not believe! Who indeed would?!

Television started here, your box in the corner, your daily dose of radiation, it was invented here Mother, by a local man, well a Scotsman really. But let us not be too particular. The Scotsman worked here in the twenties on the new invention and almost blew himself up apparently. This was the first town to host a live television broadcast, yet nothing has been done about it. Not a thing. Oh! I do think there is a simple plaque somewhere, but that is all. They cannot afford it, they say. You read it in the local newspaper at regular intervals. Imagine this in the States, Mother, the Birth of Television. One of the great events of the century. Now what they would do with that back home? It would be bigger than Disneyland in whatever town or city it happened. Millions of dollars would be spent on its celebration and no doubt continued everlasting consumerism in the great American way.

Truly unbelievable.

Never mind Mother. There is still sometimes too much of curiosity and wonder here, a warm compelling enchantment is felt all around in the surrounding air and can almost be touched.

It can certainly be smelt.

The place is not perfect and there is of course, too, the usual modern mythologies embraced by the disinherited like superstition, dogma and fanaticism, but you have them back home also. We both know that, and I am in the deep South after all!

But all this wonderful activity and without taking any of the many drugs on offer everywhere here.

I will write you a longer summary of my present existence after the carnival tonight, as I will soon need to begin preparing myself for this exciting annual event.

Much, much love,

Your own Sivvy.

CHAPTER FIVE

Back at the pathologist's palace of analysis and inquiry, the inhouse main man, bullring-born Dr. Percy Smott, the frenetic, forensic scientist of entity, with his green cotton overgown religiously spilling creases and folds, indulged in private pathos mumbling tautological references that he had a power over life as he looked down on death. Heard humming and revelling in his self penned, part finished, cacophonic tone poem, the dried blood smeared manuscript always close at hand except when periodically disinfected by clones with unlucky talents cleaning necessary surfaces.

Displaced not in this job market, he hardly had time to cruise.

> He knew
> what the few
> know
> that death
> is the freezer
> and there is
> always a queue
> to go

An expert in the field observing would notice, if this was deemed necessary, how the bodies he scrutinised quickly and professionally in ways immediately obvious and familiar, but only to him and his elevated kind, demonstrate a profound genius in this field of directionless finality.

D.I. Swettervil could have reached the mortuary sooner by travelling the same vehicle route in the hospital grounds the bodies follow, but he still could not bring himself to approach death so quickly and so candidly. His being urgently indicated waste would not wait, hence he had called in the communal, water closet on an alternative route to the chamber through the isometric pattern of polished, foreboding corridors with rooms of mystery where people are changed, sometimes beyond recognition. As he spilled towards relief he noticed the scrawlings of an enterprising scribe of the garden gnome school of fashion playing big-time prophet on the gloss painted walls.

> 'All the women came and went
> Knowing Michelangelo was bent
> A lot of young men came to see
> If Michelangelo was really free
> And would he wait for butchyboy me?'

The hand-drying machine would not activate on pushing the button. Eventual physical anger to appease the system brought no requietness. So he pondered, moved to the light switch and confidently clicked it twice. On and off. Hence the machine obediently performed to stay wind-tunnelling for as long as the situation prevailed. The wall scrawl held his vision to bleak inspiration, and on continuing to his goal a slow revision of the disclosure occurred.

While walking a rhythm cranianised and fell into a chant.

> 'All the women came and went
> all the women came and went
> all the women came and went
> all the women came and went
> all the patients came and went
> was Michael really bent?
> all the patients come and go

> all the women came and go
> all the patients came and go
> all the women came and gogo
> who the hell is Michelangelo?'

His rapid, voluminous pace stirred inner, meaningless strengths and passionate, senseless beliefs through the empty, selfish act. From his comedy mind of past fame a Tony Hancockian rap commenced, spilled out, spoiled truculence and puerile obtuseness to the empty, hollow walkways, concluding with a Jerry Sadowitz monomaniac rant, self depreciating all inner anger. Echoing to his satisfaction loud with a clarity of release along these extensive passageways. Reverberating the KKK in Thomas Stearns Eliot's original works.

Instant but bleak therapy.

Wild eyed dementia and deference roomed alongside the passageway, peer curiously through toughened, tapered, thick glass panes recognising something vital in his voice that was taken from them long ago in what was a very different world.

> 'All the women did not know
> the four cadavers in the second row
> two up and two below
> high was Jack and high was Joe
> two more stiff ones stay below
> say to Johnny go go gogo
> Buonorotti it's not your show
> how you got here no-one will ever know'

Arriving in the chamber he still stank slightly of the vine from his very recent visit to a paradise.

Empty, hollow and free. He hung there in the doorway craving originality.

Looking around he muttered to a posed confusion with himself the only audience.

"Is it love or murder again in this place, or is it love and murder? Will I ever know? Death remains as natural as life, despite removing every vestige of life on the occurrence of death."

Glancing at the rows of aluminium draining slabs with their small, menacing, stainless steel overflows awaiting every deluge of loss, every one accompanied by powerful, glinting, chromium instruments clawing the air waiting to grasp such good news. He sang the altered script quietly.

> 'All the dead bodies come too slow.
> All the live people come and go.
> Yet still no-one talks of Michelangelo.'

His right hand searching his torn, worn, green tweed, jacket pocket for a cigarette, but finding only lozenges, even though he had quit smoking some years ago. *Occasionally the urge returns, you know.* He placed one carefully in his mouth as if it was his last supper. Between the sea-front and this long backbone of a road ridged on the edge of town, where the morgue escaped notice, was enough predictable distance with hostels of happiness adorning the sides, with back car parks to reverse into, and the consequence of absorbing this local histomap as thoroughly as he ensured his part fall to grace in such a wonderland. The lean, Birmingham reared clinician no longer took any notice of Swettervil's bywardness or topped up odour. Familiarity and predictability had caused his anthropological studies in that direction to long since dampen in ardour. Eventually Swettervil mumbled but loudly, though steeped in one of his apathies, walking towards their partially covered inquisition.

"So, marks are there?"

He looked away from the physician's work, and to his surprise became aware of a radio playing too quietly somewhere back in a sideroom. His ears strained to discern the familiar pulsating background harmonies detracting him from speech.

Bill's Corpse faintly drifted in and around their words.

This gentle, coincidental, tour de force would have curled a smile in another lifetime lighting his whole being to rapture. But never in here. Never in this place of such selfless redundancy.

"Marks for all to see. As marks do. Meant for all in the fashion show of life to indulge, criticise and condone. He had a flash in the brain. Some movement violent and vital to him soon before death. That's what it's called," Percy's Brummy accent bounced around the room.

On several of the higher shelves behind them among the glass vessels of preserving solutions and cleaning materials a viewer would notice several of Percy's childhood models of mortuaries: miniature plastic animals both indigenous and international spill on to other ledges, all exhibiting ball point pen applied personal straight lines down and across torsos as on a butcher's chart showing the best cuts. Here to advertise the most successful pathology entries.

"Not very technical, is it?"

"Not everything is. If we don't have a word for it, we don't have a word for it. Medical knowledge isn't all pervading, you know...Some osteoporosis in the limbs too, he could be vegetarian. That's too much carrot juice and not enough vitamins if you're interested. His mind possessed of others, not dreaming, but pointing in their direction, like your own private night town; haggard, car-crashed and lonely. His head absorbed and inter-related some hippie mantra. Maybe a favourite haunt of his, who knows?"

"You mean he was a country boy tripping...or you are!?"

"Not so it was dangerous, no. The only heaven pointed at him."

The pathologist tried to smile. "No contest, no argument. A hook onto his kind of fundamentalism was all he needed and took."

"Psychedelic as fur on the local brew again, that's all? So anything other apparent on the naked? And what about his clothes?"

The autopsian noticed and squashed a sluggish and tentative, common, housefly, that had recently settled on his nose but had now begun to masticate slowly on the victim's dirty clothes, with a rapid, automatic, clinical arm action murmuring, "Die, insignificant and anonymous *musca domestica*!" to the executed.

As this occurred Swettervil catalogued afresh how Percy Smott's hands generally seemed much larger than his head as if all the immense knowledge the man held lay in his feelers because of their great size, clad in their skin-tight, Sherwood green, latex gloves fleetingly revitalising the dead skin on the table as they explored its dominion.

"It seems from accumulated knowledge on rigor that death the earner happened only nine hours ago; it was a blow, or rather several, viciously aimed at the back and side of the head with what seems a wooden object. Cortex flattened and broke through at several points. Cerebellum customised inward to re-route cerebral aqueduct. Corpus callosum squashed in beyond belief. Look."

Percy Smott moved away from the body, much to Fulke Swettervil's relief, to alternatively proudly show this guardian of democracy his cornered computer screen displaying the goreless, graphical-relevant, brain tissue information. The public servant observed gauchly pictorial, millimetred slices of human cells previously digitised from a self confessed, executed murderer's, full bodied, bacon slicing acquiesced to science, greedily bought by U.S. of A's P.C. companies and too credibly clarifying the specific, inflicted damage to Fulke's eye and mind and stomach, all miraculously cured of nausea.

"I...I see Percy. Thank you," Fulke admitted.

"This was unnecessarily pernicious," Percy Smott durated, "Splinters in this picked out too frequently. Baseball bat I would edge towards. More than one, too. The harder the hit the more likely the break-up of the weapon, hence the splinters. But the time? Late. Into the night. So whoever it was waited venomously, particularly to that time and then did...The clothes were scattered, some in the allotments, some down the slope."

"So it's the young at play again, or that's what we're supposed to think. But this is too contrived. And much too violently dramatic. Especially for the poor bloody tripping hill stroller...Somebody enjoyed this. Some sick twats. Still if what you say is true his trip meant that he wouldn't have known anything about it at least until the late stages ...or the last stages. I shouldn't think it's anything to do with the carnival either. Or is it? Though why by the crock of wisdom am I thinking that? Time of year I guess? Time of year. Curious."

"Yes, I reached the same. Oh, just one other thing. On one nate, resplendently graphical and not gothic but almost a tattoo to believe in."

"Where was it done?"

"Probably George Street. Aren't they all? You should get his name there, no? Why not ask what was it called, Fulke?"

"OK What was this boldface ink pushed to its conclusion?"

"Elvis is king Liberace is queer."

"Jesus. That's better than Tom Jones, isn't it, Perc?"

Both smiling widely now. Tension beaten back.

"That's even better than the Rites of Spring to me!"

"Or Chappapua Suite to me!"

Picking up on the emotion.

"We must drink to it someday soon."

Both chuckling as if in conspiracy.

"We will. Have before. Will again," Fulke replied.

"See you later in the week?"

"No doubt. No doubt."

"Still see Malc?"

"Yeah. He's still about. He'll be there."

"And Sylvia?"

"Course."

Both continued to patronise the each on musicology as their speciality.

Their conviviality shone like lighthouse beacons full on emphatically compounding under the glaring, theatre lamps reflected onto the cold, gleaming, aluminium slabs of all our futures.

Their musings gradually faded as their company gradually separated.

CHAPTER SIX

It was weeks before when D.I. Fulke Swettervil discovered a particular volume of poetry by some long ago, known variant on his level that ushered in a new, troubled stance on his usually uncluttered, subdued drama of life and love and crime and their intermingling, inevitable events. Finally home from work and enthusiastically browsing through new editions of male magazines he had purchased that afternoon from the Hastings Book Centre, a solicitor's doorway away from the Victoria Wine shop on the Harold Place junction where he had bought the single malt whisky he was sipping in his hot, black Turkish coffe.

While waiting for his previously prepared, now microwaving chicken madras curry to ring hot and ready while the Captain of all Hearts wailed ***Son of Mirror Man-Mere Man*** from the cat-scratched, veneer-surfaced speaker cabinets vibrating on the unpolished pine bookcase.

When he saw!

The open booklet sneered. Its print dared absolute and sacred confrontation.

He could not believe the deed, did not want to know of it and sat quietly for minutes stunned by the revelation. He wanted to deny it, to remove and obliterate its all.

Anything to make the action disappear.

This strange happening. A perplexing contumacy advertising too voluminously. Violent aggression into his intimate world laying below a suddenly important lacuna. A malefactor of device. His mirrored composition reflecting back at him. He had seen the passage before. A while ago.

Long years ago. Another world. Such an intrusion from that lost past life. A sub culture in which he had played a positive contribution. So he liked to think.

Anger turned to recollection of these times. Soon thoughts swam back and forth.

There was an innocence in whoever picked up who at the poetry readings he remembered, or so it seemed at the time. That was all there was, or was his mind playing nostalgia's wiles?

Soon after Pansy, his wife, had left he resumed going to these readings. He felt still young enough to have passive ambitions in this direction. Pansy was not the type after all. "No money there," she said. "No money in anything you do!"

But here the stuff is spilling out! A chance for him to make some?! It's here in someone's volume. Of sorts. Someone he knew in the past. Someone he knew very well. Someone who is right now making money and acting famous, displaying herself much too coarsely, loud and garish that even he could not fail to be aware, AND USING HIS WORK!

His introduction into a world where the pose and the belief in a sweet caucasian dream displayed, fawned on and ravished by all that entered, to incorporate merely one token ethnic of any persuasion but where none are allowed equality on their own terms, had been complete.

Some known slapper had stolen his precious thoughts, his wonderful morphemes, she could not have dreamed the same epoch epic, the same seminal, the same prolifigacy. Impossible. Nobody was so magnificent. This remembered filcher knowingly, deviantly, commonly, must have secretly taken letter by letter his private imaginings, his scribings, his personality, his whole, his total wonder away. Without him knowing.

He feverishly looked for the name on the cover and read out loud as the microwave dinged its completion of preparation. "Xaviera Hume!...You!...You cow!...How fu..fucking could you?!"

Stabbing to a theatrical death the printed pages of betrayal, he continued, "You deceitful bitch... I'll fucking kill you...I...I will."

A giddy exhibition of disorientation rolled around the floor crying and howling before a stillness.

A stillness in which the pained thought stayed long and slow and deep and thorough.

The realisation that no court in the land would give him back the rights to his work was instant. Why should they? For how could he prove the status quo? He had retired from performing other poets' work on those poetry evenings youthful years ago to instead work quietly on his own slim endeavours, stubbornly hiding the results never to be published, what with his feverish, frantic, monomaniacal, developed dread of failure. Dominating him at these times was wild, uncontrollable emotion deciphered as an inability to accept any defeat.

KAKORRHAPHIAPHOBIA.

The term for his inadequacy.

He sought it out, learnt the spelling , wrote out the literal and tore the paper into pathetically small pieces wishing he believed in the powers of superstition.

Staring out the window, looking down onto the road where a broken down car with its driver's head under the bonnet, striving for the correct assessment and sufficient correction of the problem, plays the oblivion card to the horns and curses of impatient traffic piling up behind trying to pass on this awkward dangerous corner finds him smiling again.

For seconds.

These days Xaviera made what they call waves, splashes of self selling, producing loud promotional literature, appearing on relevant television programmes, singing rap with a partially clad, squeaky-voiced boy group and using most opportunities for self publicity. She was, he guessed, still better looking than him (*wasn't she always?*), noticing again her still desirable flesh and kiss-pink lips displayed teasingly, discreet though, unequivocally pointing to private, imminent seduction for all purchasers through the well cropped, soft focus, soft porn photographs advertising the slim, attractive volume.

Plus, as much as he desired he could not repudiate the happy, confident urgency of the unrestrained language read in the triumphant prose on the loose shiny book-sleeve, but only rage to stress inside himself.

"Xaviera Hume, truly the nation's favourite poetess, is no longer a shooting star in the newcomers' section, but has rocketed to much greater orbital heights triumphing over the echolalia and spilling indecisiveness of every man."

The already abiding appeal projected onto her talented beauty and the seemingly hypnotic adoration felt through the pages as he scanned the introduction and the poems was too evident to his crushed personality.

Plus the publishing company Falbala & Fibril would automatically be on her side, as they would have no reason to act otherwise. Sickening tacit complicity he presumed. A court case would be sweet free publicity, of course. How could they not embrace it?

To her credit she had shown her land owning, rich, uncaring parents that she could manage as well as Rupert, her greedy, sometimes too familiar brother, their son. He, after all, was allowed the luxury of carefully choosing a career and pursuing it with naturally nepotistic support which he successfully accomplished and was now heap big business somewhere in the cities of his free world. Her femininity felt the stifling patriarchal bias all childhood to early teens and she left the family home escaping the cosiest way by hooking onto, an admittedly family judged secondary alternative, the lowly art school route. Aka rites of passage with hippie spiritual acts for the many inadequates, she soon became aware of, while sadly knowing the multitude expected nothing more, and felt even less she believed.

Fulke knew all this. He had known for a long time, seemingly since time began.

Her story was etched into his consciousness to the point where he could almost hear her bleating, but at the convergence of territories, on a war footing he left all this buried deep inside emotionless, to dry up. A fresh, hopeful dawn of a new, exclusive legality enveloped him. Controlled him.

And it developed with frightening, uncontrolled energy.

Now the secret rules within the Force, never perfection before or since the seeped to the press, halcyon, thuggish, dreamy days of the Metropolitan Force in the Sixties, cultivated his mind towards their usual stylised, brutal agreements of necessary, final punishments when definitive, personal involvement occurred. He knew the road on which to steer dangerously.

Behind infamous folklore he would create an answer to his predicament.

His law within the law. His law within their law. His law within his law. His law was the law.

> THERE WAS ONLY THE ONE ANSWER
> THERE WAS ONLY THE VIOLENT ANSWER
> THERE WERE NOT AND COULD NEVER BE
> ANY OTHER ALTERNATIVES.
> THERE WAS ONLY EXTINCTION.

This could not be allowed to fester like the relics of a saint.

Strong action needed to be taken. Fulke Swettervil had believed present, superficial values would protect and preserve him. He was both a consumer and protector here, and had endeavoured, contended and failed without moving; dashed on delivering the exactness of semantics; scrabbled by difference of values; he had opened himself to everything the world of dark duffel jackets, livre de poches, French cigarettes, snug pub bars and long haired beautiful girls could offer. Just a dream in the crepuscule of a craven creation...and lost - heavily.

Fulke, and his Modigliana-inspired, green corduroy suit for all seasons and all off duty hours *youthful hero reading revealed the painter always donned the same artisan keks,* had met a particular girl, a once ago, within this crowd. Somehow quirkily superior to the rest of humanity was her instinctive appeal to him. It was a special night, a professional poet evening, a George Macbeth reading he remembered, they were always popular, held invariably in the back room of some dodgy public house that ambitious, young, epicene clothed poets would never enter normally as, self evidently, material for their art would never linger there.

CHAPTER SEVEN

It happened during the coffee break.
People sat, diminutively grouped, around dirt-ingrained, brightly coloured laminate-topped tabletops, unsteady on their speedily rusting metal, tubed legs. Hunched, well worn, posing intelligentsia shoulders echoing discursive murmurings of the thinly disguised, iambic metre of the poems and feverish mutterings about the poet's beautiful girlfriend sat so superior somewhere to the side of the evening's main man. All heard between soft drinks or black coffee in this echoing, upstairs, undecorated hall normally used for budgerigar and finch breeders shows, local amateur drama groups and extreme right wing meetings. The dissatisfied few, including Fulke, chose to move noisily down the yellow gloss-painted wooden stairs for a drink in the bar below, especially when the star turn of the night was clearly heading that way with his young female consort.

When he spotted her.

She stood apparently helpless. Tight, white, short suited halfway down the stairs seemingly in some difficulty with a twisted high heel or a snapped gold ankle strap or something. The vulnerable beauty ignoring every offer of help but his. It never fails that one he discovered.

Not on him.

He enquired as to the possible alternatives in her situation and invited her for a beer or seven. She accepted graciously while the malarched footwear that normally sustained her form so correct and sublime miraculously corrected to function.

She became a goddess. Her wide moist sparkling eyes looked up and through him. "Is this the season of the stars for a young and handsome poet to carve out a wild and rebellious requiem for all Gods?" she sweetly enquired of him, sipping her rum and black.

Their metaphysical bodies had met.

He had done a reading. Of other people's work admitted. And she was impressed.

She liked his reckless mannerisms when reading verse, the way his fingers splayed mockingly slowly one by one as if calling out to particulars in the audience or speeding all at once everywhere around for substance, and his acting out of the piece like a rock act strutting the boards instead of the usual literary icon motionless monologue. She enjoyed his passionate outspokenness on the belief of genius in his subject matter at the same time pleasurably gazing on his lean, tall, straight-spined, tight-corded figure noticing failing gauntness in features welcoming time's healthier proportions. And the way his hair not quite fell onto his face.

This she wanted to know more.

He liked this nymph who smelt of the usual poetry crowd aromas; Disque Bleu cigarettes tastefully tinged on tooth-polished teeth, just the vague continental touch of garlic residue on the slightly breathless, full lipped, pouty mouth, and carried josticks in the cotton Rastafari handbag to light back in her town centre flat with the promise of stronger substances later. All and more acted with confident elitist aplomb, secure in her tight fitting, short, shiny lust that had never needed to flirt.

She adored his name and reminded him that Fulke was a Poet's name; he had passed this first important test with an 'A' plus. The only pass mark. Her sooted eye shadow, black lined eyes, long semi-fringed bleached blonde hair, mauve pastel matt lipgloss and French film star looks blew softly over her black velvet chokered neck, of a safer sweeter sensual spiritual sex than he had ever known and a joining of minds beyond and because of history. All spoke of her gentility and expected ambitions. He listened. He wondered at all this.

They had consummated everything on their one and only night at the cinema.

Of course, not to revel in the common marketplace but to indulge their elevated status, they found themselves sitting not quite alone in 'The Black and White Night of Masterpieces of the Moving Image' in the rundown, continental films cinema squashed between the outskirts of the business area and the beginning of distorted development desperation.

Their unknowing enchantment was a showing of 'The Misfits' starring Marilyn Monroe, Montgomery Clift, Clark Gable and Thelma Ritter with the winsome screenplay by Arthur Miller. American melodrama turned to high art to sell more seats. Modern cowboys and trailers and horses and guns and drugs, Reno bound with no country music. They watched the screen curiously as frail, falling actors played broken rodeo riders protected by their world, edging their ways to death acting out a collage of esoteric emptiness and still hoping and loving the camera, the machine that once loved them will offer salvation. They listened to the faked out language harnessed to the emotion underneath apparent to the film buff trained or gifted. In their continuing frightened existence these similar beings once lived only for their art but now it offered no solace. Makeup smoothed out a vanity of wrinkles but not the ones of the heart.

The last picture before life's ultimate showdown.

"We're all dying, aren't we?"

After the celluloid immortality was canned and presented the players gradually demonstrated a cohesive co-ordination of mumbling metempsychotic afterlife as they fell to their deaths public and physical. One by one. Out for the ever.

The lovers saw and comprehended very little of this as the common but so cultured darkness quickly became their habitat. Wrap around commenced as her hands gently stroked the back of his quasi rockabilly haircut to the nape of neck and horizons beyond while he tenderly approached her perfect torso. Orifices slowly began begging, insisting, demanding, pleading guidance and attention in a primogenitorial, mutated stance. They felt like the first man and woman. They were the new Adam and Eve. This could even be the beginnings of a new religion. They pivoted on the globe. This exploration, caressing and stimulation of apertures and cavities slowly transformed into the love affair of the century. This was it. It had to be. Even when the houselights came on.

They expected applause but graciously accepted sweet, silent apathy.

Undaunted, they knew. This was the event. The genesis.

He never knew when or how he had passed the full course. It no longer seemed to matter.

For a long time there was sublimation.

After first flushes of flesh, passion having sated to reflective stillness, the physical declared an equal meeting of the cerebral. Until Fulke, without consulting Xaviera, decided to become the examiner and judge; until the meaning of existence, economics, ghosts, territory and truths were emptied out of mouths and hearts and lifestyles and they were seen and heard to differ. More. To polarise. Right off each other's scales to...

He knew, as she realised and echoed, that their affair was limited to decay.

Back to her corner seat in her black duffel robe, luminescent mini skirt, and stiletto heeled short boots Xaviera went and stayed. He had always liked her name. Hers was a sexy name, a glamorous dirty name. The type of name that excited the boys before they had seen the girl. It always worked. As he watched others perform always as if in the same Greek mimed tragedy. They stopped as he had stopped, they thought as he had mused, they acted out the same theme and failed predictably. He knew the tragic lesson of the game of love had been absorbed. Things different staying the same. Always to remain. A sadness unknown came over him.

He realised she had always been there.

Still, this remained someone, lucky in economics from her beginnings had stood and acclaimed his outing. Stolen his tripped out meanders like a dog stealing a bone from a traitor's gibbet. This entreated townhouse, country seated girl cushioned by wealth and power had convinced herself of a talent that she had not, but all monies and position in her society, all in her favour would convince the world of such a rightness and exactness. An unarguable, unequivocal ultimate that told him of society's rules. The ultimate to him would be his triumph. After all if she was successful showing his work then of course it is his fame.

Only no-one knew this, so he would be without the vanity and instead with kicks in everything private. He had told close friends, the singular few, that his glory as a poet was academic. Only a matter of time and therefore was to be early home.

His picnic with the virgins of literature was arriving very soon. Every friend he had known and gained some confidence within his soul had said, "I somehow know you will be a dreamer, a maker of other worlds and a romantic novelist of your own and our world."

If not.

Felo de se was in abeyance he told them.

The final act.

But something had happened. Something not expected. He had always collected poetry books, books of sayings, books of quotations, books with different styles, language openness of values and distortions, etymological scrambled. Volumes closely, carefully, slowly opened, devalued, cryptically broken down, analysed, dispersed, segregated, expropriated, fragmented, dichoted, unassociated, broken down.

Broken down. Breakdown. BREAKDOWN! BREAKDOWN!

Issuing forth and not in control. Surrounded by this abrupt admission of plagiarism or do we discuss the differences between mannerisms and tracing? He to himself mumbled on and on. There exists the capitalist cult of the celebrity time and he wants that playtime...talented or not.

After all others get away with it.

But to read in a book recently purchased his own words, his own workings and beliefs, his own scrambles of humanity and normality labelled with another's name was a dismay to last.

Commencing with despair. Beyond mutilation, and torture, and death.

And definitely certain afterlives.

Slowly, unbelievingly, he read again compulsively and again compellingly and again hypnotically and again dumbfoundedly, and again...and again... into this long late manic night.

LOCK IN

> He does not ask for applause
> It is too late now
> Life has been played
> and lost.
> Success and women
> always felt uncomfortable
> they could make the razor blade slip.
> But here
> he is safe
> with too much security
> surrounded by his drugged god.
> I only now wait
> to achieve
> this elevated level
> of oral ceremony.

He read, he read again and he read again.

If a picture formed it had no advancement and merely haunted. How could anyone reduce themselves to this displacement of the rules as he understood them? His age told him dreams were looked into before exhuming. Stupid bastard, he thought, how could I think that an academic world could blow my dream?...

Then again, they dared to try to dampen this romancer of culture and diatribes?

He listened to the wind and rain outside his window and ***The dust blows forward 'n the dust blows back*** in his head or in his stale, curry-smelling flat.

How to do it was only the option. He felt stronger realising that.

CHAPTER EIGHT

Torment tears through him. Impossible to brake.

Like a woodsaw charging through ripe, young flesh.

Aching, panging, twinging like slow, vituperative poison.

Smarting supplementary never to leave.

He is a mess.

The phone rings waiting for recognition. Gradually the noise plays through to suffering ears.

Eventually as the ringing refuses to cease Fulke's fingers reach for the black fingered plastic.

She's too much for my mirror is very loud this seventeenth time round.

"Hello." Angry and irritated he is.

"Er...Sir?"

"Yes. What is it now?" he snaps at the world.

"Er..This is the station, sir."

"Oh it is, is it? What's your problem?"

"Er..Me..er..You...It would seem you are, sir."

"Me?"

"Er, yes...sir."

"How do you mean, me?"

"Well...er... how do I put it? Could you please turn down your er...music sir...We're er...how can I say it ...we're..er... getting quite a few complaints."

"What?"

"We're getting complaints, sir... about you!"

"What the hell are you saying?"

"It is ..er..very late, sir."

"Who do you thi-"

"And whatever else you're doing, sir."

While the station volunteer is ahead and confidence building under anonymity the big question outs.

"Will you..er...stop doing it...please?"

"What? I don't believe this. Fuck you!"

He slams down the receiver.

"Fuck the lot of you." Shouts to no-one.

Waits a moment and snatches it up again.

"And the rest of this pathetic fucking planet!" Slowly realising he is bellowing at nothing.

He fast forwards the phone to its rest and whips around for variety.

Tears out the disc player lead from its wall socket.

Plaster crumbles.

The music slurs to a silence of sound.

His flat is quiet now.

The street sounds gradually take over, but he does not hear them as he is already being taxied back to the Old Town searching for a lighted pub window that denotes a late or early morning drinking session.

He pays the cab and walks.

Around the next corner ***Strangers in the night*** is heard and soon isolated.

Middle aged women acting like girls, he thinks, giggle out the side door. Fulke successfully squashes and swims against their tide through this same boozer door wondering about the something that did not happen in their lives. Malcolm Lowry is alone in the smaller back bar murmuring something about feeling institutionalised when Fulke cursing lightly finally negotiates full entry without even noticing the name of the place.

Ten minutes later Fulke understands the comment.

Strangers in the night rings out again to the accompaniment of mal-gambolled piano keys and aged hoarse voice.

And will continue to resonate.

Of course, it is nearer, too.

The unusually stark halogenised horse and coal brasses light effect with artificial coal fires witnessed in legal drinking hours by the obligatory sunglasses worn clientele had all but disappeared for their covert session leaving just a single bar light and one other. The effect was dramatically sparse and direct to any bigot, but deemed necessary and pleasant by the two friends. The several velvet maroon quilted walls made Fulke feel they were situated inside some immense ornamental sarcophagus. The overall impression of the room whispered desperately "Only for your money suckers. Only for the money," and was, in a minimalist world, successful

"Hello Fulke. How goes your world of ragged empirical truths?"

Strangers in the night.

Again clearing the head like a decongestant.

"Oh, hiyah Malcolm. Not too bad, I suppose, and yourself?"

"Oh, I'm as fine as a harridan in hell on the opiates flowers of desire. By the way Sylv's only just left, if you were wondering. Gone home to work or sleep. She didn't know which." The epaulette brown shirted Malcolm replied.

Strangers in the night.

Never afar away.

"Yes, I suppose I was thinking she'd be here. Always nice to talk to. The best in fact. They don't come any better. Oh, sorry, love. I'm not being very polite, am I? A pint of death please."

Looking at her but smiling at the noise.

The young woman behind the jump, seeming supernaturally supreme being bathed in the crisis of chiaroscuro, serving brash light in Fulke's drink, smirks back as if expecting our two heroes to comment, curse and guffaw on the musicianship of the ivories destroyer.

"One for you, Malc?"

Strangers here and there strangers everywhere.

A move in the song's interpretation.

All feel the change disturb thought and dialogue. Addiction quickly rearranges articulation.

"OK, I'll have another whisky, Irish, of course. I'm not going back to Ripe tonight, I can tell you Fulke. It'll give the wife some small relief. God knows she deserves it. I will remain suffering in this tortured declamatory province of history's past that hasn't passed yet and shows no will in so wishing to do."

"There you are." Fulke hands him the drink.

Strangers in the night.

Like a co-efficient of overtaxed tautness.

"Thank you. I'm booked in here tonight. That's how's the bar's open you see. I'm working early in the morning. Down at the 'London Trader'. A new book. I've permission to write in the bar."

Another reason for Fulke to politely smile.

"Oh dear!" Spoken low.

And gibe. "Well, I hope you make it Malc. I really do."

"Oh, I will. I'm excited about this one. It's different from the last time. It's a mescal laden expulsion from a paradise of drunken lunacy psychiatrically interned in a Rabelasian void."

Strangers in the night.

As the tapeloop of one instantly familiar song.

"Not too serious then?" Fulke cannot resist. He radiates failed white dentures. Not wanting to admit to himself that Malcolm can write interminably well under the influence while he needs sobriety to attempt any meagre mused utterance.

Strangers in the night

A sound barrier with a problem.

"Does he get many bookings?" Fulke smiles to the bar girl and Malcolm.

"I've been listening so long I can't smile anymore. In fact, I've decided he's going to die in my new book and quite horrifically," Malcolm opines.

The girl smiles her customer smile.

Strangers in the night

Lest we forget.

"After my day and night it's welcome relief, I can tell you." Fulke again.

"Too much work then?"

"You could say that."

Strangers in the night

The summing up.

"You want to talk of the disparities inherent in your employ? Or in your head?"

"Not yet Malc. Not yet. Thanks, anyway. I suppose that means it's obvious."

"Something is Fulke. Something is."

The song finishes.

"That was called ***Strangers in the night.***" The entertainer speaks.

Fulke guffaws. A thankful discharge melting his monumental stress.

Malcolm ordered a loud Faustian recount.

The bar girl screams a delight. Her mouth opens to stream a beam of sparkling gold from reconstructed molars to light the dark bar corners.

The song slaps in again. Even at this time of night this cannot be allowed to fruit.

This piano player is a lucky piano player.

Eventually the barmaid has enough of the redefinition of entertainment, and sanctions the unique finger broker with silence preferring the low sounding jukebox to keep her awake.

"I'll buy you a drink now, Fulke. What do you want?" Lighting his speckled fawn on brown pipe as he does so.

"I'll have the same as you had last time please, Malc."

"Please doll, would you? Would you like one, too?"

"Might as well Malcolm. Spend the time productively as they say... Make this the last one then, Malcolm Lowry sir, lover, will you? Please. Pretty please?" she replies, looking him in the eyes teasingly persuasive.

"Yes, of course doll. Of course." He turns and winks at Fulke.

Finally the pipe flames independence.

"Malc what would you do if anyone copied your work?" Through thick tobacco smoke.

"That's a funny question, Fulke, because I was accused most of my life of copying others."

"Sorry Malc, I forgot."

"That's all right dear boy."

"But what if someone did?"

"In my position I don't know. Probably who gets there first maybe."

"Oh. I see."

The hesitant dawn stumbles stuttering, embarrassingly, enquiring quietly through the thin, plum coloured, closed cotton curtains. After Fulke and Malcolm have woken the fitful dreaming, loud snoring bar miss from her slump at the jump, her potential for comfort, and helped her upstairs to bed, she, between states of consciousness thanks them for their efforts, they drunkenly, gently peck her goodnight.

Fulke leaves the premises while Malcolm downs another drink before grudgingly accepting inevitable ascension and loss of control on the largest scale.

Meanwhile Fulke's spiced hot curry remains in his microwave.

The other side of Newtown.

Cold.

CHAPTER NINE

Every seaside town has one. Some more than the one. Even the most Tory minded, upmarket, home counties tinseltown has a failed portion of land that the town hall clock conveniently forgot. An area of disparity, dissent and rusted in obsolescence envious of even the nearby, neglected council estate. Permanently downtrodden and starved of funds, industrialised where the poor tend to congregate in hope, where sacrifices are many, economic and everyday and the blinkered, idealised council offices conveniently ignore most of the problems.

Subordinated in a competitive world, symbiotic to bondage and chancery, browbeaten to the bottom of every pile of pixiedust. Situated en route to a better world where vehicles and their passengers on their excited rush to the coast; "I can see the sea, look mum, look!", do not even notice this rundown through the glass scene. Today's cars shining with new coats of toxic paint from the suburbs of cities ignore these garish echoes of what they have left behind. They are too intent on reaching the contaminated beach to play bucket and spade and beach umbrella with sand and oil and effluent.

Paint lacking everything standing, permanently missing from the neglected, decaying industries surrounding the terrified, single row of bricked, terraced properties on a blind bend in the road, under a railway shunting bridge, that points the divined traffic on its consecrated direct route to the beach car parks.

Stepping out of front doors the drum occupiers meet only wood shavings from a trickle of successful factories, petrol fumes, oil and sea-water on the accelerating curved wind entering all capitulating orifices; out back entrances although the sea is only yards away nostrils do not sense the wildness and promise of a freedom as it is a long time buried behind decaying industry, privatised railway lines and new vacational movements. Vouched for idylls of sailing, sunbathing and play live there but not for the actuals, no, not for the people of this part of town.

On this disregarded crescent where at night, left fight with right, skins and pakis clash, skullheads and hippies claim a unique transcendence, white soul and rude boys make a kind of love with their violence, immigrants and nationals dispute and talk of world economics and proclaim who will suffer next; where in the day crudely designed posters proclaiming yet another mass hysteria of market forced research preferably reclaim windows from vision. Where a young white woman dragging a young child with her risks the speeding buzzing traffic on the corner and rushes across the road to this row of houses to shout 'Fuckin' paki!' and throw a brick at any window; where newspapers and milk deliveries ran dry years ago without large deposits; and where celestial conmen, wearing suits of see-through superficial superstition, walk these surly streets knocking on all doors preaching their brand of bland security where all subservience is applauded and independence is condemned.

Where all flesh is bad and all spirit is good. *If only life was so simple.*

As Seventh Day Adventists or Jehovah's Witnesses or the Children of God instinctively know.

Blank pickings are embarrassingly rich.

Here is where our moralist lives and breathes his vengeance...

Though, with yesterday's experience, the proselytisers of promises give his devil's door a rushed cautious glance and hurry on their soul blinkered purpose.

Where on the hill overlooking this busy dirty road, there is always a hill overlooking this type of busy dirty road, there lays a mound of material plenty with luckier people in smarter burglar alarmed detached houses and double garaged four wheel drive vehicles in an elevated, unpolluted position instinctively knowing they are superior.

Still picking over every point, angle and meander in the dark corners of his hurt, sensitive and confused mind, like a starving animal sucking long-gone, savoury-boned carrion, squeezing out any last negative reasons for the generative act to be withheld, Fulke Swettervil gazes out beyond his third floor bright bay windowed rooms across the overactive road with its noisy traffic to the human high carmine red spray-canned unevenly streamed JESUS IS LOVE YOU ARE ALL FUCKT on the opposite wall.

Humming to the subdued strains of **Beatle Bones n' Smokin Stones** and momentarily occupied noticing the dropped and uneaten scraps of overcooked, insubstantial, burger-shaped malnutrient spilling from a discarded, unrecyclable container, expensively sold by double-crossing, dishonest corporate business, laying on the uncleaned facing footpath, being flapped and fought over by squalling seabirds oblivious to the noise of the aggressive, relentless traffic passing, he is surprised to find himself thinking of Chekov, his sadly missed late pet seagull as he watches the irregular behaviour below.

How the young bird had initially peered into his window staring a long time day after day. As if deciding the place was sufficient for its needs before eventually beginning to peck the sashed glass for attention. Starting with post silent taps to gradually strengthening beaked blows until Fulke felt certain the window panes would break. And how he responded by feeding the persistent fledgling, caring for its welfare and allowing it the run of his flat even to the extent of choosing television programmes by wing displacement. How the squawking squab knocked relentlessly every early morning, whatever the weather, and if Fulke was not there would wait the day long until he appeared and usually with some titbit for the bird's supper. Expensive foods were purchased for the winged wonder to eat and the bird somehow communicated its appreciation of these treats or so the male nurse believed. And how the bird would mustard foot stomp on the soil for minutes on end until an earthworm would rise, pleading for the quiet. At which point the gull would obey in its suck of a swallow of the intruder.

Heartbroken, he painstakingly cared for the careless creature on discovering his pet had been savaged by a young fox and almost, but suddenly not, surviving the attack. And how, as if to reclaim the reality of Chekov or to help his special grief for his failed feathered friend, he started out with predictably fervent obsession meticulously building a three times larger than real scale, papier mache model of his pet. Using thick and thin metal wires to shape the armature, balsa wood curves and shapes to amplify limbs, much coloured tissue paper, quality gouaches and clear varnish he completed the accurate, frozen in flight, construction. Everyone seeing it commented on the impressiveness of the model, his toil of affection and respect which still hangs from the ceiling in the entrance corner of his flat. The only object he regularly dusts.

Now another sadness.

Thoughts tail-spinning to an uncertain death.

Man made God, and in Man's image, and not the converse he knew. His ego dictated. So loud. So feared. When there is nothing to fear. So much hope. When there is no reason to hope.

The stars on the United States of America flag, displayed as part of an airline advertisement on a large billboard viewed obliquely along the street that cars notice before they crash in their only true celebration, appear to him as Ku Klux Klan puppets excitedly dancing in their uncertain void. He reads again the rouged words of the feverish, fundamentalist fanatic and articulates that man fights for anything and kills for nothing: the incorrect use of the name of a place or a man loving woman hating deity, a territorial line only over which some may be permitted, a flag standing for nationalism or an advertising secret society, a world-wide body despising religion that is the only truth, a people eugenically superior or a limping racing greyhound are all valid reasons to manifest mutilation of the masses. The crazy half truth they call passion is not his way and never will be. Stupefaction settled in satisfied still waters merely floating feebly in brain cavities.

The capitalism in which he lives, slaves and eventually perishes, accepts without a murmur his failure to copyright his work and consequently allow, no, unequivocally advertise for, another to steal his labours.

A shift off all duties and all he can do is dwell on the counterpoint of fame or failure.

Another black coffee. The kettle performs with steam. Bent forward breaking off a portion of Stilton from the customised, dented 'fridge to eat with his snooker ball sized onion bhajia, his nostrils inform how his appliance has begun to smell like the appliance of everyone.

Stale and alien.

Thankfully ignorable, hence forgettable, with the door shut.

Embarrassing when open and anyone is around and familiar.

Somewhere a bomb, planted by young believers and constructed by shamans, liberates energy to destroy innocent women and children, reports the distressed travel reporter on the pine kitchen shelf red plastic radio, and a politician says how bad this is, when all know he paid the ferryman.

Fulke no longer hears these foreseeable familiarities of man's grand design; instead he continues to watch his animated, chewing face, attempting improvised face exercises in the mirror for some moments while spilling out crumbs of food.

Stroking his chin he wonders about shaving while looking towards the soundless, large screen television boxing clever, but sees right through the tube. The considerable image denotes two middleweight boxers sparring to truth with one naturally winning. Fulke does not notice the champion's face exhibit anguish aplenty rather than show time joy as he uppercuts to knock out a brother. The champ knows the white society's rules and the lip service it shows to other winners. He plays the money game while Muslim brotherhood guardians patiently attend.

Fulke's gaze moves on. An irrelevance as nothing is witnessed.

"Cucumbers categorised according to curvature."

Between relentless mesmerising bouts of muzak of uncomprehending blandness, the radio continues to play more European Community chants of conformity and presumptuous insanity.

"Anything to fill the spiritual vacuum. What?" He bounces back at the machine.

Braincells active again.

Digestive juices attack the fromage and hot chickpea centre slowly absorbing into his system.

He reaches for the orange juice-full milk bottle on the table, removes the mostly aluminium top and drinks the liquid greedily hearing it rush down his neck to leave his throat out of sound.

Normally he appreciated these two, strong, distinctive tastes mixing to an occasional oneness during his deliberately slow salivation and he enjoys their polarising moments when each taste piques the other as in a revenge, as when the cheese would flood the bottom of the mouth while the spiced onion flavour would acrobatic the roof of the mouth and on into the nose, and the warm stomach satisfaction when finally swallowed. A comfortable residue.

But today... Problem dominates taste and thought.

Elbows on the window sill he passes still more time gazing down on lives already wasted in underachievement, missed out on all but the free butter and tinned meat until...

CHAPTER TEN

"Free Willy! Free Willy! Free Willy! Free Willy! Free Willy! Free Willy!"

Human beings are nothing if not original.

Shouts of a freedom. Or from a cage.

Slowly approaching becoming louder.

Beginning with a phrase commercially exploited fully, burnt out, used up, slanted, moved over, a mere sideways step from one expansive continent to a smaller proud realm. From celluloid to street. From film to reality.

And the shout renews, mutates, transforms on crossing the globe.

Of course it does.

Loses any possible projected idealism to reach a crasser street level.

Moves from a mammal to a bird.

But. Another Willy?!!

Sounding nastier, too, the loud noises presently heard in the street below.

Fulke gazes down on large crowds of demonstrators mulling along the road like a crazy line dance of segregated resurrection. Ready to condemn anything in their path.

Banners held high proclaiming *'Freedom to Willy the White Crow'* and showing a white bird on a black circular background. All wearing badges advertising this persuasion.

The ubiquitous Socialist Workers Party placards are there too proclaiming *'Let Our Indigenous Wildlife Go'*.

Shouting. Chanting. *"Free Willy! Let Willy the White Crow go go!"*

The mob still swearing and singing and threatening others.

Car horns hooting private exasperation.

Traffic slows to standstills before and behind the wavy, unsteady flow of people.

Drivers leaving vehicles to implore the banner carriers to move out of their way are told this is more important than anything they could possibly want to do. Conservatively dressed motorists leave their vehicles to hit fringe garmented and patch jeaned hippies who hit back.

Providing the hippies did not hit first.

Blood splats onto knuckle. A face echoes the colour.

Daubs of disposition depressingly sudden darken walls and tarmac.

Fulke notices only two coppers with this five hundred plus strong, heady crowd of mass hysteria composed of right standing middle aged women, loose lipped young anarchists, planet idealists, occasional day trippers needing a sudden buzz and do-gooders lodged in between.

Sadly, slowly, predictably in his policeman's mind, all getting out of control.

Massing road and pavements. Winning control of the street they travel.

Someone blows a trumpet tunelessly. A distorted guitar sound is heard in the distance.

Knocking on car windows happens. Stickers are pushed through sunroofs.

Excited and large back seat dogs bark and squeal, jump to the front seat, on up to the sunroof. One dog is successful and has left his car to chase and growl after a particular unlikeable demonstrator. Dog teeth nipping at the man's jeans as man and dog disappear round a corner to hopefully forge peace.

Stickers are planted on neglected shop windows.

Free Worlders becoming aggressive when told to move on by trades folk and car drivers. Scuffles break out inside/ outside/ around and about surviving shops.

Car windows are broken by some hot-headed, velvet jacketed long hairs that Fulke recognises.

Families cower in vehicles. Frightened for their lives.

Babies cry. Women and children scream.

Some fight back. Deliciously.

"It's those fucking animal liberationists again. I wish someone would set them free!" he half-heartedly cursed. "Give me football hooligans anytime! What I'd do for a couple of sabre toothed tigers now languorously wandering down this street! That would clear 'em, I bet! In more ways than one! They'd soon grovel and beg for those cats to be destroyed when they'd watched an arm or two ripped off and playfully freefalled in the air before becoming supper!...And I recognise two of the thuggish bastards down there! I'll get them all right!"

He rings in to inform of the trouble and suggest more policing to this march. Now or sooner.

"It's worse than Northern Ireland here. At least they only march to history, ritual, religious bigotry, supremacy and territory as only they see it!"

The phone listens because he has superiority.

"But what do we get? What do the morons march for here? It's not their precious veal calves or bouncing sheep or free range chickens. No. Not that simple. It gets worse. Much worse. It's a fucking albino bird. A white crow would you believe? Still, we have to be grateful for no racism in this, I suppose! This pushes the Northern Ireland six county treks into the second division!"

As he remembers the newspaper article skimmed yesterday with the front page photograph of a white crow, under the article about a dishonest politician, protected by the RSPB who passionately believe the bird will be killed by other black crows for being different if released in the wild. And the accompanying picture showing a militant Mother Earth group set in a country clearing around a comforting camp fire that believes the bird, *like all God's creatures,* should go free and will go free because they say so.

"But what are they doing here? I know it's this coast they've marched along before, but nowhere near our town?"

The phone is dropped.

On his side.

He continues to scorn the mass of humanity out of his window.

"Presumably they're to meet a counter demo?" He believes, but does not communicate this information back, thinking surely they will calculate so also.

The whole mass of noise and irritation gradually fades and sways away uptown towards the rusting pre-renovation pier.

A lone, stumped honey bee worker *apis mellifera* stands on and stares at and through the closed, top window pane debating the abrupt, profound density of air. And is it personal?

Fulke looks up and notices the failed creature.

Thoughts move to Sylvia and her poetry of the working insect. He remembers mortality statistics seen at the station stating that forty people a year die in Britain alone from bumblebee stings and shivers in and around.

Sound diminishes to return to the usual hum humdrummed. The trapped bee adding to the drone of quietness. Back to solipsistic selfishness in this muted discord acclaimed as stillness he returns.

Everything inside has concluded. This is it. The finality before the completion.

His decision has been made.

To stay the dignified act out. And punish the thief.

He gazes across to the red wine-stained soft-wood bookshelves on which stand his painstakingly garish coloured, cartoon strip version of 'The Greek Mythologies of Superlative Western Thought' and knows...

He is not to be caught. He is never to be caught.

Not like his favourite, mere immortal Sisyphus pushing a superior, heavy boulder uphill for the remainder of time.

But to be trickier than the omniscient king of Corinth and walk away and allow random sands of life's inefficiency to run through still strong, thick veined, sensitive, age showing fingers.

To remain a logical positivist philosopher and not a tragic mystic, and overcome others' deaths more than the twice to forever endure cautious liberty.

To remain free and dispose of all Aresian competition; and rename the shitty boulder! *If all else fails!*

Endless and ineffective. Never.

If discovered in his necessary private retribution and made to work with stone, so close to stone, locked in stone would make him stone in time. So a form of Peace would result.

If sentenced: to push, to shift, to motion, to exert labour as an ideal.

So he retained belief in the self hence to verify and accept whatever the outcome as fear of punishment was never his worry.

Yet he repeatedly failed to notice that the modern, graphic illustrations of the ancient God pushing his particular boulder up his personal slope resembled too closely an anonymous convict working on his favourite rockpile. And that this dot to dot, shaded in convict had a particular close resemblance to himself with his square shoulders, pale face and wave of hair forever falling to forehead.

CHAPTER ELEVEN

Fulke and Bo met at a party.

Semantically concurring a formal civic gathering that transformed into a party in his mind. The big bash given, as he found out later, at her parent's residence.

This pompous function was a Sussex Police and South Coast Councils arrangement with Rotary Club members, Winkle Club attendees, shady extreme politicians of every party, a few genuine public servants and various public benefactors craving titles and positions. Something to do with security in the suburbs and fighting off the poor, and he had to be there as a representative of the all resourceful, regulating force and to inject unruffled realism at the same time as squashing hysteria in the social and probable antisocial proceedings.

He had been out most of the day. Preparing himself.

Drinking the world dry.

Usually he told others he was questioning potential suspects or doing undercover work or waiting for the tip off of the decade or alternatively all three. A trine of declared deception. Not particularly caring how people saw through this or conjectured the waste of public money, as he knew these other people were permanently irritated by his undeniable success rate in tracking criminals and jailing them.

Dusk was performing affectionately when he discovered himself in a house alarmed sprawl dedicated to the righteous celebration of wealth and inequality. Through mind mismanagement he had arrived at the address of the night's gathering too early. Standing outside the grounds of this building, looking for all the world to him like some high class, freemasons drinking club; large, turreted, balconied, expensive stone, mock-Tudor sections, with semi circled aggregate driveway onto four garaged site. He wondered his next move.

There's unquestioningly booze in this dump, he thought as he walked up the long curved drive and there's certainly not a pub in miles so...

The only choice was to knock.

Someone was heard waddling to the portal.

Fits and starts and structural shudders gave way to the beginnings of jarring.

"Wha' you want here?" The door was noisily and slowly opened by a loud voiced, small, middle aged, double chinned woman in yellow curlers and a loose, green chenille dress disguising steatopygia sympathetic thighs. She had bare, red nail polished, recently washed feet he noticed as he listened carefully to the instantly sobered eloquence of this charming stranger's plea.

Before he could speak.

"Of course you can come and wait in." Her East European accent was beginning to soothe him. "It will not be before long others will be here I should imagine not." The eroneous speaker sported a nose foreshortened to mundanity when looked fully on but a proud angle of ethnic beauty glimpsed in profile.

Fulke, thanking her graciously and thinking how her accent reminded him of mother and home, warmed immediately to her immigrant manner. Inspired, he bounced up the entrance steps of the suburbs built, mock-old country house and after tramping through many thick carpeted, long, purple lurex corridors was shown with a syntax stricken, emphatic finality into an auditorium laid out too lavishly with food and alcohol for the gathering.

"I am Mrs. Viall am I by the way, but later you call me Bunny maybe. When we know each better. You can stay here if you so wish and you yourself help to a drink to all them. But you will excuse me, and my husband of course too who does not know, as we are not quite yet, you see, ready to join people as others and yourself." She spoke softer this time and smiled beginning to approve of this young man yet not knowing why.

"Thank you for your understanding, Mrs.Viall. There should be more like you." Fulke believed the words he spoke, though noticing how her second chin ended on her chest reminding him of a farmyard cockerel, how her thick browned skin had obviously been out in the sun too long promising mid-life melanoma and how her nicotine stained yet perfect dentures caused him to consider wealth and its uses.

"That good. Oh, thank you!" the lady of the house said and disappeared through one of the many doors to change or transform, cook or juggle with smokers toothpowder.

Before standing back to study this arena of compromise and luxury, he sought out the drinks cabinet coquettishly hiding in a recessed corner disguised as the all pervasive DIY blockboard Beerkeller Holiday Bar perpetuating sobriety through in-built crassness.

"Are those poncy coloured lights around that ...that make believe jump shaped like a swastika at Yuletide or is it me?" he wondered before speaking to the plenished snug.

"Don't be shy, you wonderful conspirator of illusions."

He had been instructed to help himself to drinks, and for once his usual contumacious nature failed to protest.

"My nickname could be Bacchus for all she knows," he muttered, not realising that some people at the station already call him titles of this persuasion, "Though with her act she's probably nearer to it than I am."

Singing tunelessly, "I was lost, though wise
arrested by your lace curtain eyes
crowded by your garden slab sighs
but now I'm in a heaven called Paradise."

He poured himself a large glass of his favourite Bushmills single malt whiskey, and was enjoying sipping this fanciful, Fenian fluid while nosing around this spacious hangar covered in green velvet-embossed wallpaper curtailed with glass cabinets holding figurines in various domestic postures of both frightening blandness and expense, staring away from all tragedy.

Noticing the games area, he carefully picked up and held a blue snooker ball off the mauve cotton-covered slate like a rediscovered Yoric, his mind instantly swimming fondly in recalled earlier minor league snooker success. His cerebration hit intrusion upon hearing peripheral scratching, progressively mounting wide of sight, and looked up to notice that a dog, a slobbering quadruped of astonishing energy and dizzying development, a genetic flaw excommunicated from The Kennel Club, a massive, ugly Rotweiller the size of a pony with a stretched head, slavering leer dripping from the side of its mouth and paws as big as novelty carpet slippers, had moved into the far end of this boundless locale from he knew not where and its white, sappy, staring, runny eyes had settled on him.

A solitary, vertiginous dog flea *ctenocephalides canis* bungee-jumped out of the animal's recently shampooed fur to lose itself in the thick carpet below. Obviously into textures and out of soap.

With a psychotic mixture of curiosity, malice and paranoia this Baskervillian creature indolently sniffed the air offering a stare of fatalism and ferocity to its potential prey before emerging clearly to run crazily, but straight, and methodically towards his confused mortality.

Hands still sustaining empty glass and snooker ball, Fulke stood and waited irritatingly decadent while the tyke, with no intention of diplomacy but obviously to lunge and tear deliciously at his face on contact, confidently surged closer.

He commanded the approaching animal to abruptly cease its unsociable behaviour but, not being police trained, it just kept on coming.

The glass and ball were rested.

He called again but still it raced. Striding longer and stronger now. Body muscles changing shape. Like lemonade bubbles spilling from its jaw. Energy oozing out high and low.

As man's best friend made like a jump jet Fulke was instantly back in the Forces, he fisted the confidence from the wide slobbering mouth and with a loud falsetto squeak of surprise the beast thumped the carpet noisily and slipped away on hunched forelimbs to consider this new challenge to its territory.

Fulke poured himself another tall whisky and checked his ex-Royal Marines knuckles for damage. They held adamantine.

He looked down, sat down and twiddled with an executive toy, like an executive.

A shiny metal ball swings through the air on a twine to hit the first of a line of balls. The opposite end ball in turn swings out through the air while the first ball rests with the line. The second ball returns to stop on hitting the line of balls and the first ball begins again its predictable journey.

Why do they bother?

He became rapidly bored, dismissed chaos theory, and thought again about snooker.

Minutes later the pooch returned to the room ruminating, as dogs do, in corners and lower regions with only a hazy, disappearing memory of their shocked meeting. Consequently on scanning its immediate horizons a form corresponding to a stranger met its gaze, and alarm bells rang again somewhere inside its grotesque frame. The cur commenced its ritual sniff of the air, slowly transforming into take off run speeding up ready to leap and try again.

"Come on then, you dumb bastard, if you want some more." Fulke stood and melodramaed.

As the mutt rotated, Fulke, exasperated, smashed it with more conscious force this time, a power shaped to an end and the hound floated and crumpled to the floor with a pathetic, shrill whelp and a long sigh. The creature's eyes popped out with its jaw closed tighter than prebirth, displaying a quizzical look on its face that was previously worn by the first human. It scooped off at speed several seconds later on waking, shaking its head bemusedly.

Undaunted Fulke carried on inspecting the room, browsing on looking at the first editions of gold braided medical books like 'Elementary Surgery for the Bourgeoise', sailing magazines still under cellophane, D.I.Y. encyclopaedias, cookery books, racing driver biographies, Geoffrey Archer papers on modern philosophy and Edwina Curry volumes of literary criticism in the teak bookcases. On a hardwood table near the large Carrara marble fireplace he noticed a family portrait, here was Mrs. Viall with her rich husband and smiling daughter noncommittally staring out like a less-fat margarine advertisement. He picked up the gold photograph frame, began to ponder and stare as he slowly realised that Miss Viall, though some years older than Jackie, his daughter, exhibited a very close resemblance to her and he was slowly becoming aware that he found this Miss Viall compellingly attractive. Pondering on the nakedness of this new thought, he looked round for any other pictures of the Viall offspring adorning the room, possibly showing her at any younger age to check this theory. He noticed and lifted one, a photograph in a spiky edged silver frame off a cabinet of gold and glass, showing the girl in her school sixth form hockey team smiling proudly, suggesting a special cup-winning day.

Now doubt had ceased and confirmation begun its slow methodical exploration of the facts so far. The similarities became definite to his eye. Thoughts developed. Thoughts like...

Was this it? Was this what Pansy sensed? Was this why she left, and not my always working late and drinking? How come I never sensed it then? Because it wasn't there, that's why! Because it was always her! Always scrawny her and her budgeted attitude to her and money! His money!

It was now ten minutes or more since the enterprising canine last attacked and Fulke's memory of their ruckus had almost faded to blank, controversial new thoughts sensationally taken their place, when the animal mustered up another assault.

There was no need to turn on hearing the now familiar, slow, deliberate, manic shuffling. He comprehended all. All he needed to know.

And this time he was more than ready. Rapidly becoming too ruffled by this sad annoyance, he wanted it out of his way once and for all. A desire to drink and think swept through him. Old dreams and new. He was enjoying himself, on his own, in this chintzy manor, with old thoughts and new, before all the respectable crazies appeared to create the convention.

Next he was to beat his own best in a billiards game.

But before any of that he had a mission to conclude.

The dog drew on all its strengths, pounded the floor, sniffed at the air for guidance and inspiration, sighed and commenced its run right across this long room. It moved faster this time, picking up more speed as it came, as if out of the very elements of life.

"You sure you want this, you fucking overgrown rodent? Come on then! Come on you bastard!" and the dog obliged. It kept coming.

Bounding along in a fast breathing rhythm, a dramatic belly sway to each side, regular panting as it moved, coming closer and closer. Tail and head down to increase all aero dynamism.

Clinging to the belief that speed was its friend and lover too.

The animal lifted off. Again defying gravity. Ground cushion effect existed inches below the now stretched muscular body and snapping phlegming slavering head soaring towards Fulke's neck.

Closer, closer, closer.

Stilling himself, Fulke prepared for the final confrontation, waiting seconds longer than the previous encounters in that before moving he did not smash the animal down as it left terra firma, but waited some milli seconds or so watching its whole form spring, feeling its energy and sensing its warm, stale triped breath salivatingly near.

Then he acted. Grabbing it by the bullet head.

"Gotcha now sunshine!"

He dragged its pate towards the floor and commenced to pummel it methodically, angrily, relentlessly against the carpet, gradually edging it towards a skirting board where the brute could expect more pain for less effort and many times cursing it to hell and further until it passed out for a few seconds. Fulke stood over it like a virus. The dog came to again, only to be pummelled further. He laid into the beast until it eventually became still. And stayed still. Breathing steadily as if in sleep.

When the dog woke minutes later slowly recognising its surroundings and with life's lesson now definitely absorbed, Fulke was enjoying another, quite drink. The deflated critter sneaked a frightened, remembered look at the relaxed victor, recognised its Sword of Damocles and wandered off in a determined, straight line to disappear from his world as soon as possible.

CHAPTER TWELVE

People arrived and greeted him accordingly depending on their power, selfishness and capital interest. He smiled the smile of the wise and convivial, easy in these surroundings, chatted politically correct and exuded his careful, caring persona democratically.

The hall feverishly filled with the rich, the uncharitable and the avaricious, plus partners.

A few stood apart, afar and aloof, shuffling apologetically and beaming bombastically at the gathering and each other and the ceiling and walls in turn, awaiting their time to harangue the rest into arrogant conviction. Their throats fastidiously cleared to tuning fork precision. Pompous, neat notes on colour co-ordinated, fake stone backed leaves scattered on and off and about the provided South American hardwood, one size only lectern.

The populace watched and waited. Someone shuffled louder than the others and began.

The chest medallion-clad Mr. Rufus Rust, the pharmacy chain owner, after much rustling of beard and bracelets and dropping of green veined papers, droning with the liberalism of an Orangeman marching through a Catholic estate, commenced with his frenetic symposium on how hard drugs hurt the underclasses by stopping them from working, getting them into trouble and anyway how can they afford them.

Mr. O. Mould, the bank manager, after some relocating of papers and sickly sniffing, his small stature looking round the ambo, continued the thematic, eugenic line, whining that the poor are very bad economists and a recent, right wing management survey concluded that most of them can hardly spell the word or many other words for that matter.

Police Superintendent H. Putty, in round shouldered uniform, drawn and tall, not one of Fulke's favourite colleagues, falling forward over the lectern with large police boots barely holding him upright and only squinting at his notes, confidently reminded everyone that the police force meet a certain type of person daily, and that these people always claimed total innocence of any crime even before being accused of it, and not at all like the rich who always help the force no matter how inconvenient to themselves.

Big Rex Viall, the prefix permanent because of his massive business, wide, bald head, enormous dog, flash car, large, portly frame and booming, unrefined tenor of a voice, the owner of the big pad, and a baldness that was more Welsh mountains than South Downs as the hair climbing around his large ears would never again seek the peak. He patronised of never too good security for and from everyone, which was instantly acceptable as all knew he ran a successful security business along with his long term thriving scrap yard ventures. He fully realised the problem of what colour to choose one's individual, customised house burglar alarm box and what problems this could cause the purchaser, but please check the paintwork colour on the building and go ahead regardless.

Fulke drunk pathologically along to these pathetic, woeful comedy turns until, distracted by the last speaker's long blond haired daughter playing the perfect hostess, wondered about his main act of the night.

He gazed in tenderness and unselfishness as the young woman met her grandmother and old aunt placing her arms around each and smiling as she pulled away to say, 'That's nice,' gazing down on their garments, "It really suits you!" The aged accepted the warm comments, converted them to vanity and stored happiness inside.

As these tired dialogues of selfish guarantee demands and police state patronage dissolved into the back of memory, the spirit of bacchanalia warmly and gratefully reappeared suggesting possible opportunist openings he would not waste in the usual manner.

The party was in full swing, the large music system softly suppressed a bland disco version of ***When I see Mommy I feel like a Mummy***. He had, with the aplomb of an Old Testament prophet, attached himself to the beautiful, begotten baby of the family and had steadily developed a crave for her misbehave, a hiding for her biding, a tingle need to mingle. She likewise felt her emotions amusing his the longer they toiled each other's mind, and they toiled. They were true toilers. Of the heart, and the body.

They desired development.

The colossal bronze cardigan, light brown jeaned and swishing, dark brown cowboy booted Big Rex and his beloved, the shiny, green top, white sheen ski panted Bunny with her loose fitting, mushroom ornamented chain belt could not fail to notice this flowering of passionate, cerebral agreement, blind oblivious enrapture and stark lust, as apparently had the whole of the inquisitorial guests, and were consequently wondering whether to allow its full, natural development and any possible consequences, or disengage the couple with a finality that only money and/or power can successfully accomplish.

The whole room of snivelling onlookers could not help noticing that their beloved daughter seemed to want to talk to no-one but him, which was so fine by his way of thinking. The couple discussed each other's tastes in music, theatre and life and found plenty of agreement, she asked about the job and he found pleasantly to his surprise that she was soon to work with young offenders against and with him.

Fulke mock pleaded with her not to refuse him as he would be forced to seek out a parallel universe where on finding her delectable double he may be luckier.

She smiled with caution aware of his intake.

His eyes met a hippie fashioned, conservative, bright yellow locked beauty spilling out of a liberally pastel flowered, short cotton dress freckled flesh all over the place. Inside and out.

Sweet soothing spots before his eyes.

While she looked on attractive, black haired, dark blue wool suited, narrow bottomed slackness, experienced manly shoulders holding dandruff specks in check good figure, undefined discipline and genial libidinous, erratic behaviour with a touch of desolation she could tame and manipulate.

In time.

The white shirt to offset the physicalities of hair decay she realised, on watching him remove his dark jacket quickly brushing the shoulders as if no-one could see and placing the garment safely down to chair level, where it was picked up by poorly paid staff to hang carefully behind and away from the action. She told him not to worry as he looked aggressively towards the quiet polite remover of his jacket. This is how things are done, she said, sensing the words would calm him. Placation is power.

This was one of those meetings to change an individual's life. Or two individuals lives. Again.

A loud ignorable growling coughing noise sounded. Interrupted most minds.

Everyone but Fulke looked towards the cause.

The dog had escaped from the kitchen and moved towards the now silent, horrified crowd. Slabbering and wheezing, wild eyed and growling obviously irritated by the throng.

The parents panicked in style, distraughtly so, suddenly aware of living in the litigious age. They called and tried to stop the dog unsuccessfully, frantically and commenced resigning themselves to the fact that their hound was going to damage somebody or something very soon.

The dog, not to disappoint, bounded across the room, as people shiftily flowed opposite, in its now familiar gangly fashion wanting to clench its newly ground dentures into human flesh. And noticed a weakling.

Turning it stopped and sniffed the air.

Standing and waiting the victim was suddenly aware.

The dog bowed its head, pawed the floor, dribbled a saliva well onto the carpet and slowly commenced picking up the necessary speed to maul.

Mr. O. Mould, a previous speaker, a small, balding, bespectacled, flaky shouldered bank manager comprehended all and tailspun into terror. His eyes watched the sweaty creature coming closer. One hand clasped his groin while the fingers of the other rushed to his mouth which began to make funny, helpless noises eventually converging into a sustained whine. "Eeeeeeeeeeeeeeiiiiiiiiiiiiieeuuuuuu-"

The hound sprung.

All was quiet.

A lifetime of silence slipped by unnoticed.

At that precise moment Big uxorious Rex realised he loved the dog more than his wife but refused to declare his decision to anyone ever.

Mr. O. Mould was hypnotised. And now quiet. Even his dandruff hovered.

"STAY!" boomed over the event like a deity.

Everyone turned away from the dog to gawk at the omnipotent voice.

The loud voice of presence and command.

Fulke's voice of presence and command.

And experience.

The dog, confused now, appeared to hover mid-flight, divert, windage shot, cough a little and sail, legs wide to the ground. The animal slowly rose to its paws looking around quizzically.

It panted a recognised smile to his master's voice, licked his hand then satisfied left the room wagging a praiseworthy tail.

All together or one at a time.

"My hero!" sighed Bo.

"My bloody dog!" said Big Rex.

"My g.g.god!" squealed Mr O. Mould.

"What the-?" spoke someone else.

Mr. O. Mould had relaxed. Sweating and shaking and sliding down a wall slavering onto the voluminous expensive carpet.

"Portillo has never done that before. He just did what he'd been told. Did you see what? I said you should get that dog down put." Bunny ventures to her husband Big Rex.

"Who let the bugger loose? That's what I'd like to bloody know. Who let the bugger loose? Where's that bloody gardener? Where is he? He was supposed to be bloody watching him. Where is he?" Big Rex perplexed.

The room still stood amazed. Motionless. Speechless.

They all gradually looked and moved towards Fulke.

"And you must be a bloody genius. That bloody dog has never done as it's told ever since we've had it. I don't know why we keep the bloody thing, and how did you bloody do that? How? How?" Big Rex calmed, came and offered his handshake to the local hero.

"Thank you Mr. Viall." Fulke courteously took his firm grip.

"You can call me Rex like the bloody rest of 'em. "

"He must be very OK good for our child, our little girl if he has such magnetism, such clever."

Bunny confided in Big Rex.

"You must be very OK good for our child, our little girl if you have such magnetism, such clever."

Bunny turned to Fulke.

He smiled back at her. *She sounds like childhood revisited he thinks.*

People began to clamour round. Congratulating him on his party piece.

He wanted to escape. He needed to escape.

Someone eventually remembered Mr. O. Mould still shivering, now snow shouldered, sat on the floor. Fulke followed over to assist. Any excuse to move. Anything but this snivelling sycophancy.

But the in-crowd followed him over to the frail one.

Now everyone helped up Mr. O. Mould, who could not stop stuttering thanks at Fulke as soon as he saw him, and sat him on a comfortable settee where he was given a strong, brandy cocktail. Soon he could speak without a permanent stutter, but some silences between sentences would remain for a long time to come.

Fulke, not knowing what to do, escaped and began to move back into the room towards the bar .

"That could have been big bloody trouble you know. I'll kill that bloody gardener when I find him. You mark my bloody words," Big Rex said to him as Fulke's urgency caused them to almost crash into each other.

Hoping he would not be held to such a confession Fulke had greater reason to keep moving.

"Another whisky Bunny!" Big Rex bellowed past Fulke's ear while turning towards it. "And thank your inspector too while I remember for giving me the address of that burglar that broke in here." Fulke tried hard to vanish away from this embarrassing masonic flavouring, and even desperately considered hiding behind Bunn's ample backside when she eventually brought Big Rex's specially imported whisky.

"I'm gonna get that bastard burglar, I am. Naked on his knees in front of me. I'll have him!"

I hope you'll both be very happy Fulke wanted to shout but Bo appeared in his sight stimulating corect convention and hugged him smiling a beam. She had the prize. She knew.

"You're a hero." She smiled at him.

"No more heroes, don't you know? They're all conmen with illusions." Fulke slipped back into his reality but found himself instantly wishing he had not.

"Tell that to your fans! Here they come again!" She smiled back, waiting for the inevitable crush.

The in crowd were back. In force. Back-patting Fulke. Fetching him drinks he did not want.

Having all deserted Mr. O. Mould, who now sat lonely but comfortable drinking strong brandy cocktails just that little bit too fast.

Bo long suffered everyone's repeated congratulations on Fulke, before strategically pushing through the excited, surrounding swarm and leading him slowly and deliberately away on into the long, cool, darkened, inside locking, plant dominated conservatory to privately donate her unique physical slavery to his imperatives.

For now.

CHAPTER THIRTEEN

"Zoomoomoomoomoomoomoomoomoomoomoomrr rrpphhhh!!!!"

Dank, dark, terrifying dungeons where failed cloning experiments and the mutilated mad swear, slabber and sweat.

Omni-dimensional in a cabal of diabolic, depraved virility seething in a seeping plutonium purgatory, post nuclear landscape where decapitated, still squinting devils and death defying zombies patrol.

"Boomboomoomoomoommoomoomoomoomttttthhh!!!!"

With his sword of enchantment, poisoned delayed exploding crossbows to anti ballistic missiles and magic potions of invincibility and longevity in this other time, in a far away kingdom where evil persistently counterattacks white goodness forever, Galahadaggedon, the unvanquished hero of all sweetness and radiance and right wing correction techniques with his faithful shield Tumult protects his pure chaste being, and ours self evidently, wrestling with these eternally overhasty, dynamic, pernicious enemies.

"Dundundundundundundundundundundzzzzzhhhhh!!!"

At this moment, in their near and far dimension, in their everlasting span of anti-mattered existence the mother of all battles rages.

Vindictive and spiteful as any last judgement.

"Wapapapapapapapapapbbubububububbbbbuuuppp!!"

Tumult the impenetrable shield yet again reflects Archangel Zaracuda's torpedoes back onto his grotesque, hunchbacked defiler, who explodes gloriously in slow motion wrenched flesh *as many times as you like*, noise and colour spilling all around to interminably evaporate.

"Rutututututututuutuutttatatatat!!"

A million more of Zaracuda's troops are dispatched to their netherworld by Galahadaggedon's sidewinding, surface to surface, seditious swordsticks.

Awesomely high at having won level 577 of 'Crisis Icis Multi Mad Monk Mania' Albert Huddle looks up from the hand held play station, refocuses mind and eye to view a stern looking policeman appraising his stance.

"It's only Lucozade!" The bright, cheeky, wide white grinning, fashion conscious, sawn off rasta hairdo yelled through crushed up, oversized jeans, too large, hooded jacket, personal stereo and woollen Rastafarian noddy cap to the not much older, smart, creased, blue uniform and badged lid who supported Carlisle United and a wife who would not let him keep a dog.

Upon realising he had been caught urinating in the longer sidegrass while engulfed by his game this precocious, voluminous lad decided to pre-empt the policeman's question while D.I. Swettervil, tempting twine, walked defiantly over the West Hill between a small group of kite flying enthusiasts towards the still enclosed, potentially clue-ridden area.

"And I've lost the bottle!... As you do!" This teenager, this Albert Huddle concluded in the glorious happy tones of a confident, secure, family life.

"Get his name, will you?" D.I. Swettervil shouted the distance.

"Bring the dressed up garden gnome here. He might have seen something." To anyone.

"I'll slap him with the bloody bottle. So I will!" To himself.

Remonstrating loudly concerning his rights the struggling youth was brought by the same ambitious patrolman, on the same shift as his earlier appearance, to his leader.

"Don't touch me! All right I'm coming!"

The earlier dreams of this lawman now slowly evaporating. Visually.

"Get off me you..you bastards. I saw the Rodney King video! I know what you lot do!"

"Stop struggling and swearing you obtuse, melodramatic shit. What's your name, or to put it your way, what do you call yourself under your hood?"

The lad suddenly looked ten of his flabbergasted seventeen years.

"I'm called Skanker. To my friends...Only to my friends. Under OUR hood! What do you know about the hood? How did you know what we call ourselves? How can you?"

Albert unsuccessfully protects his sub culture by spluttering consternations.

"It's my job to know things...Isn't it? Look. 'er Skanker. I'm a friend. I'm a brother."

A startling silence holds.

"And take those damn headphones out. You can't hear with those things in."

"You ain't no brother! You could never be a brother! You ain't no brother! You're more a fu... more a mother! You're not like me! You're not like us! And I am hearing you aren't I? See!"

Resigning himself to the undeniable biased powers of the police he switches off the tumultuous techno rap tape, neatly removes the ear sockets and places the machine parts gently in a large pocket of his vast jacket to zip up with the shrugged finality of acquiescence.

"And you ain't no brother! Definitely!"

"Finished? Hey, as far as I'm concerned we're all the same. OK? We're all people."

"We're not! We're bloody not! Understand?"

"And I thought we were supposed to be the bigots, not you lot. I say we're all together all the same and you say we're not. We're all human beings, no differences, all born the same way so!"

"We're not!"

"OK. Maybe not, if you want it that way, but I could be a very good friend, you know. I could be a close friend you know. Too close."

Mock threatening to the juvenile.

"This is how to do it, Pile," Swettervil smiles to the patrolman standing near.

"Yes sir. I...Yes sir." P.C. Pile affirms brokenly before turning away and frowning perplexion.

"Look, all I want to know is whether you and your sophisticated friends, 'er brothers if you like, saw anything or heard something about this." His arm moves around the Hill.

"Heard about what?"

"About what? About what? Look!" He points. "We all know about what!"

"Maybe I don't."

"And maybe you do."

"And maybe I don't."

"And maybe you do..."

Both naturally tire of repetition.

"And maybe I don't."

"And maybe you do."

"And maybe I don't."

"Look...How long we gonna keep up with this?" Swettervil smiling through tight teeth.

"As long as you want," the youth replies.

P.C. Pile's facial muscles entertain a new shaped skin surface. His eyes stare.

"So did you see anything?"

"Wouldn't fuckin' tell you if I did know."

"Wouldn't fuckin' tell you if I did know." Apes his speech. "So you do know something."

"What if I do?"

"So tell us if you saw anything or anybody." Spoken slowly.

"Why should I?"

"Because we need the bloody break that's why and because we can also lock you up for withholding evidence." Exasperation beginning its inwardness.

"You won't do that. You can't do that...Can you?" he mockingly shouts.

"I thought you'd know! Course we can! That's why I said it. Now do you understand, hey?"

"I s'pose."

"So? Anything?"

"Pardon?"

"What? Is there anybody inside? Did you and your mob notice anything yesterday?"

"Well I did see some..."

"Some what?"

"Do I finish or what? I mean..Some people!" In exasperation at adult rashness.

"Bloody cheeky kids walking around looking like garden gnomes."

"Bloody impatient adults driving around looking like teddyboys."

"Oih! Steady. So it's twentieth century fashions now is it?...You were saying?"

"Me? So I still exist? Oh, thank you. At last!"

"Get on with it, will ya?"

"Well some fishermen types, but not really, if you know what I mean? They had that sort of fishy look but.. Only two of 'em though, but not from here. Not our 'beachboys'. Hadn't seen 'em before. Only yesterday they were here. They were on this hill. Scruffy as well. Drinking and smoking but looking around nervous too, you know? Like they were looking for somebody that wasn't there. Looked very suspicious. Even to me. Never mind you intellectuals!"

"Watch it!"

"Maybe they'll be around the Old Town tonight. They weren't drinking with the dossers though. Definitely away from them. On their own. Why don't you talk to them? To the dossers?"

"Look, smartybloodykeks, I'm supposed to be the detective here! And anyway I won't get any sense out of them will I?"

"You're asking me? Or was that rhetorical?"

This reference led the eye to the bricked, sheltered, seating area where a coterie of soap sparse, alcohol smelling victims of society sit and drink, and shout and cadge money from cagey passers-by.

A cabal of thirst drenching in the morning sun.

Fulke looked across and shook his head at this open example of man's inhumanity to man.

"Go and see if you can get any sense there will you, Pile? You never know."

"I bloody do though," Pile thought.

"Yes sir," Pile said, Fulke hearing just the begrudged tone of his voice.

Again to the youth, "So what's making you smile Albert?"

"No diplomatic strengths yourself huh? Hey! How did you know my name?" Skanker's smiling countenance swiftly transformed to quizzical gesture.

"Because I do! Aahh! They teach you kids far too bloody well these days. We should go back to the old days when you peasants knew nothing and brains didn't think because they hadn't been trained to," Fulke exasperated more.

"Ending a sentence with a preposition? Dear, dear," said young Albert in teasing tones. "That's accepted now, isn't it? Aren't you a peasant as well, or are you different to everybody else?"

"Jesus Christ!" D.I. Swettervil looks at the sky. "He sounds like the master race when he gets going. I give up. Go on. Sod off." He smiles. "Let us know if you see them again. Thanks for what you gave us. Go do your homework...If you've got any."

Walks away and begins to jog.

"I'll have to won't I?" Skanker turns and bellows back while running.

"Why do you say that?"

"Because you wouldn't be able to do it!"

He sprints from sight slowly until a street corner dramatically confirms parting.

Lost again. D.I. Swettervil knows.

It hurts, but do not let on to others.

"Did you learn much there Pile?" D.I. Swettervil innocently enquires.

"Lots, sir. Quite a lot," P.C. Pile truthfully smiles back.

CHAPTER FOURTEEN

Silence stands between these two guardians of western democracy as they stand watching the highway while two minutes pass modestly.

Young teenagers heading westward on their way downtown, deliberately walk across the street slowly, contemptuously, again and again in front of only speeding cars travelling down the inclined Priory Road, thus causing the drivers of the vehicles to take drastic remedial action, to the youngsters chortling amusement.

D.I. Swettervil shakes his head.

Inside is silent prejudiced thought.

Both sides of the street currently packed with rows of maldesigned vehicles sporting ostentatiously scrawled, garish number plates, and misshapen and more-shaped humanity dawdling and rushing in restless anticipation of the coming night's events. There is an excitable urgency felt in the air only surpassed by last present shopping on Christmas Eve.

Even these two agents of the state can sense it.

Merlin, Pinochio and Batman hop, skip and trump down the hill accompanied by a concealed Lady Godiva, Mr. Macawber and a two legged Lassie to their exact, parading floats. All notice a fritillary of majorettes about to prance the sea-front below in micro skirted, cute fascist, marching order. A car alarm touchingly scars the air, momentarily competing with the cries of the gulls echoing a similar territorial stance, almost off-lining a speeding skateboarder in his head-phoned celebrant world following dangerously close to a car driving down the hill.

Our protectors cannot help but notice the different ways the public treat their transport, as they witness one man micturate down the side of his declining car in the belief that no-one will notice, *not even the metal he rusts*, while another gesticulates and commands his whole subservient family from the oldest in-law to the youngest born to change their footwear before entering or leaving his pride and joy, his new expensive gleaming toy of self deceit.

A tight skirted, high heel shoed, young female plays football awkward, inferior and restricted with her soccer crazy, scorning, skinhead family and friends seriously scoring around her. They fail to understand why she does not respond to their cries of, "Fuckin' useless bitch!"

Unnoticed, behind the lawmen, a drunk sleeps on the grass as two young boys gently tip their canned drink onto his face hoping for some reaction. The drunk occasionally donates a hoarse splutter. The boys swiftly rush out of reach. Keeping safe distance.

"Just look at 'em, heh, Pile? If they're not making love to a football team or dancing to some despot's dangler of a promise or wanking over a lottery ticket, they're hanging around the south coast. My south coast. My beloved south coast."

Melodramatic louder voice climaxing emotional truth conceals full passion.

"My beloved south coast town. My Rotherham by the sea! Except their football team's better than ours! Why don't these malconditioned bugger off somewhere else? Give us some peace then we could legalise our distorted statistics. Send the sods to Bexhill, Rye, Dover, Blackpool, Keith, Wigan Pier, Orleans, New Orleans. Anywhere. Anywhere but here. Anywhere... Oh, and book him will you!"

Swettervil points to the reliever while suppressing his own physical and mental impotence at not being able to catch and book those kids for anything.

Not again, P.C. Pile thought, I'll never get promotion booking urinating utopians.

"We're lucky here while our caring politicians don't decide to build that motorway up to that big, bad, sophisticated, beautiful capital city of ours. Which means we stay provincial, and provincial with a very large P. That's the way I like this town, and it keeps a lot of riffraff out, you know Pile, this way." Swettervil continues his theme.

"Yes sir, I do know," P.C. Pile answers wondering whether his superior officer will notice he gave the wrong answer.

"We have enough riffraff of our own as it is without importing more of the troublesome shits. Christ! Our statistics would definitely dive then. Doesn't bear to wonder where they'd stop either! Oh, and you better talk to him. He may have seen something."

D.I. Swettervil points to the driver of the dog detritus suction machine, displaying a large imaged SCAMP on its flank for instant recognition and a small lettered ' Suction & Cleaning Alleyways Mews & Parks ' below this, weaving his way around the eventually faecal free hill.

"You know, Pile, some of the stupid bastards out there think that machine there swallows small dogs whole."

"Yes sir, I do. We've had to interview people for throwing rocks at the driver. He was off work for weeks because of it. I blame it on the gutter press."

"There was even someone on the radio insisting it happened Pile."

"Yes sir, I heard it," Pile quickly replied to prove he too listened to radio four.

"And guess what town she was from Pile?"

"Er, this town sir!?"

"What a world, hey, Pile? What a sad fucking world!"

Pile thinks.

Pile thinks it is.

"And them." Swettervil points to the dog walkers. "The rich ones, the trendy ones among them. They don't use dog leads like the rest. Expensive leather dog leads and chains. Of course not. They use dirty, twisted, seemingly found pieces of old rope as superior, hip, dog leads. Even here the poorer pay while the richer get away with it. Have you noticed?"

"I hadn't noticed sir, but now I suppose I will."

"And how some drive miles to this green space. To this green space." He nods to the suddenly sacred ground. "Merely to let their dogs defecate here. Come up here in a morning and you see hundreds of 'em. All at it."

"I hadn't noticed, sir."

"You will now."

"Yes, I will now."

Both look on ahead with no thoughts transmuting between.

Seconds pass. Time's only talent.

"Have you got a pound, sir, for a cup of tea?" a sleeper rough politely enquires of them.

"That's for you, Pile. My cue to leave I think."

Swettervil looks at his wristwatch. "I'm off duty now anyway. I'm going to be anyhow. Ring in and tell them to arrest anyone that could remotely have been involved and question them bloody hard. Someone might break, arrange for my vehicle to be taken back to the station, will you, Pile? I'm..er...going down Old Town to see if I can learn anything."

Pile cannot suppress a narrow line of a thin smile and Swettervil notices.

"A problem with that?"

"Not at all, sir. Oh, and enjoy yourself." P.C. Pile is one of the few that knows that his boss, off duty, continues trying to solve cases whereas all others see is an abundance of drink.

"I will. I will. Don't you bloody worry."

P.C. Pile waits until his superior is out of earshot heading towards the Old Town decline and turns to a more youthful uniform with his smiling eyes and lessen lipped grin saying, "Klens! We should set old Sweating evil a puzzle."

"Should we, by god? And what puzzle would that be then, Pile old boy?" P.C. Klens attempts a mocking accent that does not work from his mouth.

"An Old Town puzzle."

"I'm still listening but I'm not hearing."

"An Old Town to Newtown puzzle."

"So it's a moving puzzle, is it old boy?"

"Of course it is. He has to walk through Old Town and walk into Newtown without passing a public house. Without going into one licensed premises."

"That's bloody impossible and you know it. For anyone, and especially for him."

"Is it? I don't know. I've never tried it. Have you?"

"Well, no old boy."

"So nobody knows then?"

"No...and he wouldn't use it if there was one."

"He might."

"You going to give him this puzzle then old boy?"

"Of course not. Are you?"

"'Mmph!" Klens swallows loud.

They continue to watch the detective disappear out of sight.

CHAPTER FIFTEEN

Relief relaxed facial features as D.I. Fulke Swettervil left police problems on high, on hold, to commence The Steepes downhill slope, noticing Old Town roofs, brightly displaying mustard coloured moss in the stark sunlight, through gaps in the glorious, ruddy, shrubbery borders as a grin pushed through his previous grimness.

Fulke felt the pleasant complexion change and consequently did not return any wave or farewell foolishly proposed to him from the top of the mount. Halfway down the narrow, stepped Salters Lane, the second leg of his descent, his awareness of crowds massed at the bottom on each side of High Street, a long, thin, high, overpriced, terraced byway of paramoured elegance, where latent heat and dead heat occasionally mix behind closed doors and foppish diction took the place of local dialect years ago, was acute. He sensed their animosity, their discord, their vanity and their proven inability to shut up.

Relaxed, believing it to be already too late for an intimate drink in any bar, he reached the mass of thronging, smelly, selfish, expectant, heady humanity that had taken their concentrated positions outside every public house along the route of the carnival procession awaiting the event. His large bulk, nevertheless, pushed unselfishly, smoothly and curiously towards the nearest of these bars. Deceptively delicate, he moved through the crowd, his need dictated and proclaimed the approach.

The 'Filofax' tavern doorway pressingly negotiated he was happily, suddenly, inside. Diffused, limited light transformed the inner chamber to a seductive, husky, disreputable duskiness he recognised to adoration. Bright sunshine to stay out and never proclaim new dawns in beautiful, dark corners like these. If this held he would never leave. Noise, he realised, had also not spooed through into the enchanting gloom. There was a silence here. Outside heard as muffled mute. The bar was empty, bar two too close. Most pub furniture had been removed in anticipation of high profits and portable, physical decor hastily hidden away from drunken thievery. Now he could think. Not comprehensively admitted because his annoyance at drinking out of a plastic glass clouded too much. Tonight no barman would listen to any parochial review or political stand or a knowing of the landlord's ways. These asides held no power as all must carry this modern vessel of failure. He drank. His loud, thirsty gulping slowing on marginal satiation until the two tastes started to play on his tongue.

Disturbing, death rattle, gullet noises from the middle aged couple at the end of the bar prevented him making any decision on flavour dominance, because now is romance. The pleasant side of bigotry. He turned to see the dour, dainty dyad hygienically devour a pickled egg from their corresponding ends with the delicacy of new born cuckoos spilling none. A togetherness hatched in acetic acid. Their touching, crumbed, slobbered lips to clumsily kiss long and deep in triumph before looking around for an appreciative audience.

Bar man and Fulke rolled formation choreographed eyes.

The consequence of this accolade of etiquette forced him to return outside to mix with the anarchic, unhinged, abandoned, waiting congregation.

Adults stood with plastic glasses in hands, some fuller than others. Some spilt, some swore. Creaked, child necks looking up and pleading for the universe and everything sweet and sugary contained there on their terms were occasionally attended, though not without reordering another father's shant. Fulke knew there was a chance something may be noticed in all this confusion. He crossed the empty road that posed as a dividing line between two warring tribes, squeezed through the staleness of old perspiration on the new side, tumbled over wheels and footrests of unseen pushchairs, escaped dangerous flag-wavers, to eventually be prudently positioned on this higher level pavement donating clearer chances of bad blood sightings and coherent thought.

Initially the throng of faces merged as a single, blurred unit of dumb fanaticism, but gradually he began to pick out sizes, forms, facial beauties and pre and post birth flaws on individuals. He nodded to some acquaintances though others decidedly different necessitated a stare. Everyone looked guilty clearly because everyone was guilty. Always. About something.

Being a policeman he knew.

A harsh trammel of competition, boisterousness and cohesive volume dominated the wind as the carnival floats' walking pace finally commenced crawling up this highway. People were ready. Ready as ever after hours of waiting while child controlling, grandparent soothing, other half placating and all for this resolution. These crowds clung to tacky, indiscernible beliefs having read newspapers of political status dubious to him. Judgement he did not donate. This was a new world to them. It meant a dream to some and retirement to others. It spelt a journey into vitality and a semblance of freedom. A time past claiming little entertainment.

A transcending, yet disarming jollification reached each ear as people prepared themselves for this communal confessional. They were soon to shout and praise and throw some of their wealth to the passing elements. Enjoyment hung on Fulke's pertness as he smiled after finishing his drink, instantly reasoning the receptacle's tangibility as it imploded in his grasp. How to dispose of the parts? On a doorstep neatly. He caught sight of Skanker, and obvious friends of his, looking to him like failed seconds duvets at a last minute sale in their squashed in, oversized garbs of unnatural brightness. From the actions of the group it seemed obvious to Fulke that Skanker, who surprised the policeman by greeting him with a smile, was a natural leader. From Albert Huddle's angle, for an adult and particularly a copper Fulke was not too bad. In fact he was better than that. He swore unashamedly - a bonus; he drank, that was obvious and he seemed to understand something of life and its problems from Skanker's and the hood's point of view. Not that Albert would ever admit that to anyone.

Now the festivities pass our protector, approaching and passing slowly, seemingly accompanied by a dangerous rain of coins. In each direction as far as any eye can see this state of slow pacing movement with innumerable floats will take several hours to complete.

Another drink would not be out of time he decided.

He instigated the desire and continued watching.

Floats of all sizes, displays pulled by horses, by people, or lorries depending on the weight and the concept and the expense and the ambition. Themes ranging from King Arthur to Spaceman and Spacewoman and all androgynous states in-between, Peter Pans aplenty and Huckleberry Finns singular. All with scratchy sound effects to enhance or alienate further. Some held in near opprobrium while others attain heights ecstatic in belief of superiority. For this show is not for the crowds, for the locals, for the children, for the handicapped, for the television rights, for the newspaper photographers, for the holidaymakers especially picking this carnival week to be in the town: but a fight to the populist death for the smallest detail of authenticity to be studied and wondered, for the float crews to flaunt their cleverness, for the competition to be so strong that the populace cheering shouting and donating are an irritation of the worst kind. All that matters is that the judges smile benignly on their float; that they are knowing of the amount of time and effort and love the group bestowed on the project, that they have the intelligence and knowledge to ingest their obvious greatness. That they understand the universe as the members know it and will applaud them so.

When the boredom from watching comparable floats had dominated every cheap desire, Skanker squeezed through pulsating bodies to dash over the busy track between mobile units of yearlong created splendour, his friends remained eventually to refrain from watching him. Round to the policeman's position, to stand like a lost Stephen Dedalus awaiting knowledge, he manoeuvred, to socialise and glean opinions. D.I. Swettervil spoke in concepts more agreeable and relevant to his young mind but did not offer any drink, which may have been the single dominant inspiration for Skanker's original move. After some time, some floats, some donation throwing, some praising of talent and labours, another shant was purchased but only for the legal of the two. Skanker, disappointed but still communicative, pointed down the opposite row of faces to a skinhead he had seen on the hill the day before who, as far as he knew, was not local. Tall and unshaven with a cannabis leaf tattoo on his thick, muscular neck, white vested as a low suds soap advert and wearing soiled, light blue tracksuit bottoms and military boots. The instant suspect stood watching the ritual holding a partially-full, half pint plastic glass.

"Worth a check, I guess," the already active copper said to the teenager, not recognising the figure's profile in the distanced farrago of faces as he disappeared down into the flotsam and jetsam and Lewisham weekenders, stepped below thinking it would be nice to wrap this one up this quickly, but knowing it don't come that easy. Surely?

Jumped down. Pliant into the parade space. D.I. Swettervil slips between South Sea Islands and Blues Brothers floats but finds the going much tougher on meeting the throng on the opposite sidewalk. Slow but purposeful, politely pushing past a language teacher and his latest, young, foreign conquest, heavy into what they call conversation, he edges towards the indicated figure. The white vested, muscled crop still stands holding his half-full, half pint gazing uninterestedly at the procession, until the clamoured, complaining, confusion that D.I. Swettervil is generating, causes him to look in that same direction. He notices, with instant, extreme paranoia, that the copper is heading his way.

Craving first function, he violently throws his still-charged glass in Swettervil's distanced direction not caring as to any other destination and hitting a balding, bearded, wheelchair attendant on the anchor earring as he does so. He commences a visionless charge away from the confronting chaos that the solitary Swettervil is provoking, presently realising that the crowd is slammed all around him to the extent that parts of the gathering are hemmed in, despite themselves.

As the suspect endeavours to liberate himself from the stagnant, directionless mob D.I. Swettervil, having noticed the chased culprit noticing him, is noisily nearing to his target and gaining confidence at the cost of disturbing the huddled, cautious populous.

The fleeing felon tries to anticipate a direction where acceleration of self would be possible, but negotiating through the multitude of mankind is not easy and never will be. With positive persistence, he reaches the road to run up the steps of a mock-up traction bus, slowly moving with the rest of the cavalcade. He looks back and down on reaching the top step at his panting pursuer before speedily sliding groundward on the opposite side to rush into the adjacent crowd.

D.I. Swettervil apes the movement but loses his prey.

Looking frantically around, neck muscles straining and swivelling and until several voices and hands shout and point back where the detective had previously travelled, he, too, notices his quarry behind him. The sought after sinner passes several, slow-moving side-shows to obtusely take the twitternised jennel, south side of the 'Filofax' boozer, and races down it and on through the car park, disturbing loudly, suddenly and unretrievably, a relaxing game of petanque and its provoked players. With the pursuing detective seconds behind and unavoidably creating a similar atmosphere with polished, shining boules spreading still more wide and disconsolate. Ben Flied, the considered wrongdoer runs straight across The Bourne, the idle, main drag. Free of carnival and mainly deserted. Without considering deflections off metal.

But cars do screech to a halt.

One of the tricks they do best.

Seconds later different cars trace the deed as again tyres depreciate angles when D.I. Swettervil plays his mortality and despair copy.

Once safe from moving metal, Ben Flied, the probable crook turns left, choosing the inland route and rushing up the off-road crack paved pedestria to swiftly, sneakily offset his pursuer by right angling to alley up All Saints Street direction.

Ahead he slows, seeing the block of crowd lining the procession route at the end of the long passage and knows there is no breakout there. His fanatic follower, closing in, eyes the move with irritation, not criticism, as the two touch on violence some way up the connecting, narrow path. Swettervil thinks of a rugby tackle, but only to dismiss it as he hops a leg forward to successfully unsteady his prey. Ben Flied falls to grab a steadying wall rail and eyes being close to the ground spots a thick tree remnant which he grasps gleefully. Balance returned, Flied the villain aims the solid branch with some strength remaining at Swettervil's body hitting him on the neck, misting to weakness his tiring being.

Feeling successful, the transgressor decides to run back down the path over the vanquished to The Bourne, but turning left this time towards the sea-front on the clear walkway. Paved areas on this parade-prohibited road are still empty with everyone being at the pageant of flagrancy. Ben Flied runs back over the infrequently trafficked freeway to try the narrow, deserted Courthouse Street lined with fashionable, parked, rubber wheeled still lives of man's technological folly, noticing ahead yet again the restless excitable mob, this time on High Street.

Meaning no quick escape.

Looking back over a sunburnt shoulder he does not see his recovered pursuer, yet knows the sleuth cannot be far away so he crouches down to hide between the stone wall of the terraced buildings and a gleaming, motionless automobile on which some contemporary artist had scratched **Chelsea FC** viciously but artistically into door panels. One second. Two? Swettervil slowing, rounds to the street to pass the recently icon incurred vehicle. He stops to ponder his success and hears a car aerial vibrate to spring an echo on the empty, narrow road behind. Turning he sees Ben Flied shuffling off back down Courthouse Street, across the little used primary thoroughfare, to jog up the Courthouse Street continuation and run straight into The Smallest Kite In The World Man who, until that point, was doing good business, but is suddenly, irritatingly, picking up small kites. Ben Flied swiftly apologises to this man of symbolistic wisdom who stops collecting up his pennants and tries to hit the dodging side-stepping crook. He ducks a punch to run ahead towards All Saints Street. On noticing a gap in the masses he accepts.

Comfortably waddling along with the procession gives him time to think. He decides to hide in 'The Lord Nelson', the next boozer positioned swift right as he passes the chokingly full 'The Crown' public house, knowing enough souls will cover him in there, but he never reaches this safe-house. Instead, being exhausted, he stumbles left into the path of the playful activities to find himself suddenly, dangerously, in front of two grey Dales ponies, who lead a St. George and the Dragon float, causing one of them to anxiously rear and the other to promptly follow a tight tracing of this physical hindside.

Interrupted grace.

Gaits gone and fourteen hand frames poised in two legged triumph over gravity, terror glints in the sudden, spectrummed sunlight through long lashed eyes below flaxen fringes. Their sweat dripping, proud, brawny bodies pierce neighing stabs from wide, mealy muzzles as nostrils steam claiming fog as family through a sustained stance of suspension.

Each animal encouraging the other to fester unrest.

Two proud heads of gleaming, steaming energy ending with tails airing devilish streamers. Angular stance redefines equestrian balance while caressed velvet muscles in strong, stressed hind limbs extend to emphasise through a physique that metamorphoses from carthorse to thoroughbred Arab.

Life in a four leaf clovered field would never involve this.

Hoofed knock felt. Ben Flied falls.

Excited, crushed crowds on both sides of the controlled thoroughfare almost stumble and fall under the wheels and the hooves of the float and the steeds. One flank looks into blinding sun presenting silhouetted images of ceramic reared models on a middle aged mantelpiece counteracting miniature might, while the opposite pavement is offered close clarity with the visceral and the violent, visualised and smelt.

Below all the hypnotised hysteria, under the high panicked hooves, on the quiet tarmacadam level a smiling, calm Malcolm Lowry, seemingly oblivious to the clamour, is observed sitting on the road, as if picnicking on a battlefield, talking quietly and patiently to a tired and gradually awakening, drowsy Ben Flied. No-one any longer appears to notice the state of the perturbed ponies because now the whole carnival populace gawk, including the too drunk to care and the too young to know, to remain transfixed, in dormant temperance, staring on the two conversationalists. Though the sleeping, one eared, three legged tortoiseshell cat in the leaded bar room window of 'The Crown' stretches, seeing only sweet dreams.

Stillness brisks to motion as everyone's tired vision moves away from the calmed chaos back to re-engage in the supreme banalities of life and carnival. And leaving experts to peacefully lead the excited horses safely away.

Slowing down temperaments to retire the recent sensationalists to sober stud.

CHAPTER SIXTEEN

The two deposited men fail to see or hear the panting detective arrive to gaze down on them, both being selfishly involved in a private reassessment of character.

Ben Flied, the unfit felon has weakened briefly having witnessed the cheval's scared gleam in the eye and felt its tender hoof clip his fragile skull. The potential villain's shoulders ache, too, being gripped maniacally by a garrulous Malcolm happily sprawled between path and highway whom D.I. Fulke Swettervil trips exhaustedly over.

While the detective's breathing is slowing to normal he straightens up to wonder at the successful wordsmith. In his enthusiasm to communicate his story the writer is unaware that he is grasping tightly the wrongdoer. D.I. Swettervil hears Malcolm describe to the now distraught and wheezing, chain smoking criminal how he had been on a day trip to Calais, with select literati naturally, and they had congested their overloaded, returning vehicle with vessels of strong alcoholic persuasion. The custom officers, inclined to zealousness, naturally noticed the transport and brazenly accused the happy party of imbibers that they, themselves could not possibly consume all the booze the custom officers could see. The travelling pen-pushers, not wanting to add disrespect to the already hostile scene, politely insisted that all the intoxicating beverage was for their personal consumption only.

"Ben Flied. We were fucking outraged. Don't you know?" Malcolm passionately sat in dusty brushed denims and explained. "How dare they accuse us of not being able to drink our own hooch. We are Englishmen! Some of them were not! They aren't always you know! Especially these days! The insignificant slappers! What do they know? And they wouldn't let us go! Well! Not with the drink! They kept on insisting that we were flagrantly lying...we!...and our pleas sounded as believable as Bertrand Russell resurrected to life as a chanseur of the Tamla Motown soul kind. We had no fucking choice. We were trapped by insignificant clones of government. European and National! What ever they said would be called the truth later, so what could we do? Hey? What could we do?"

Ben Flied, the permanent failure in life, finally wide awake at this counterpoint in the story, could only listen while his head slowed from spin to former stabilisation.

"What could we do?" Malcolm continued echoing through the chary one's head. "They stood like bedpans of fortune thinking they had us for booze smuggling. Fucking laughable, what? They clearly did not recognise me, for instance. Not a damn clue. Not a bloody hope! If you do a job like that, of course, you don't, I guess. So, guess what happened, heh? Guess what happened. Can you Flied?"

"Me?..I..I." Flied troubled and looking round at the D.I. approaching

"We had no choice. As far as I was concerned they had defied my manhood. My life and beliefs as an Englishman were agitated by these damned lowlifes...Hey? Are you all right?" Malcolm suddenly lucid noticing Flied's nervousness.

"No. I ain't got any blow on me. I ain't. No." The febrile Flied spoke looking immediately behind him at D.I. Swettervil who was now inches away.

"You smoke the reefer do you? That netherworld of the giggle and the distortion. Haven't touched it for years you know...You don't have any do you? But I digress. Well we drank the whole pissing lot right in front of their tiny...squinting...incredulous eyes. They just couldn't believe it. They're not the type of people who could believe much at all. Much of anything. It disappeared down our throats at a good rate I can tell you. I...I was the only one who wanted an encore. Can you believe that Flied?" Malcolm queried.

"I can, Malc. I surely can," says Fulke Swettervil now standing next to both and grabbing Ben Flied's arm behind him.

"And as for you, shithead!"

"Don't 'urt me! I ain't done nofink! I told you, officer, I ain't got no drugs. I ain't got no blow. Nofink. I ain't got nofink. Well just a little. Only for personal use though, 'onest. It's only a piddly sixteenf," Ben Flied pleaded. "I ,ain't done nofink. Not lately I ain't."

"Shuttit," D.I. Swettervil gruffed a voice thinking, he's probably right if Malcolm knows him, and anyway this seems too easy. "I know you don't I?"

"Dunno. Yeah. I was on that march, the one about freein' that white bird that shoulda bin black that gotta bit outa hand."

"A bit out of hand? Is that all?"

"Yeah. Well, I was arrested."

"Surprised, were you?"

"Well, yeah, I wusn't doin' anyfink."

"'unno. Because I was bein' chased I s'pose."

"And I was doing the chasing. Shame. Do you always feel guilty?"

"No, but I know I'm always fought to be guilty. Always bloody picked on by your lot! And fo' nofink! 'nd I 'eard 'bout the killin'. 'nd that's not my game, you know that."

A wider than usual Noddy and Big Ears float forces them fully onto the pavement.

"'Know that, do I? I certainly do because we always pick you up for breaking in to honest people's property, don't we? For giving good, honest people nervous, insecure temperaments for the rest of their lives so that they find it difficult to sleep because they think some nasty twat like you is always out there. That's what you're fucking good at!"

"I-I-I used to do that but I don't do anyfink like that anymore. When was the last time I did anyfink? Hey? I always wear this bright blindin' shiny yellow jacket these days that yu' can see for miles so everyone knows who I am and where I am so I can't be breakin' in somewhere if I'm seen wearin' this."

"You're not wearing a jacket!"

"Oh yeah! ..er..Well it's too warm today innit?"

"Go on. Piss off! Before I practice some police brutality on you! And don't let me see you again today!"

"T'anks officer, t'anks. Really. T'anks."

"Don't forget I could still book you for assaulting a police officer,' Fulke returns sternly.

"Yeah. T'anks. er..Sorry 'bout that."

The sleuth lets him walk away soon to be lost in the folly of festival.

Turning around. "So you, too, know each----." Malcolm had also left. He smiles at this disappeared carouser of the old school and hung on thought, I'll no doubt see him later tonight.

Well, it's not that one 'cos Malc knows him too well, D.I. Swettervil ponders, turning round to shamble up All Saints Street, jostling through massed holiday makers, to the safety of the back room of the popularly misnomered 'ReichStag', to drink and check for minor pathologies on his body acquired during the chase and tussle.

Much later in the evening the lawman's colleagues witness a bacchanalian glow emanating from the back room of 'The Stag'. Gazing deeper into the wondrous, back distance light they discern the long arrived, comfortably settled D.I. Swettervil who, dragged from his thoughts of the night's earlier frank conversation with friends, comprehends to surprised, grinning astonishment when informed that young Skanker carried on their investigation long after the procession of floats had dispersed for another year by walking down, with his excitable friends, to the loud carnival disco held on the sea-front walkway, Winkle Island and noticing someone else in the heady crowds he had seen on the West Hill the day before.

The narrative loosened as more alcohol was offered the newcomers by their immediate boss and gradually the exploits of the broken nosed, light curly haired figure in Skanker's memory were related. How the suspect appeared dancing aggressively and very drunkenly in the orange street lighting with clearly only a matter of time before, yes, it's happened, he's picked a fight in the disco's moving laser lights with two, exuberant, po-going drinkers, much bigger than himself, searching for the same instant release.

And behind these squandered human energies. Monuments to spent stamina.

Darkened buildings with inviting shadows sagging with knowledge, looking on the lack of it.

To gaze again on another stage enacting reassessment of values.

Under a misty moon resembling a wrenched off human ear, Skanker studied the choreography of the intermittently lit rumble, even admiring J. Small's tenacity taking on these much heavier boys, as he appeared only medium and wiry. Further surveying of the indistinct, sectioned scene proved J. Small could handle himself in the sudden free-for-all with the two invited heavies and their uninvited mates exploring the boundaries of persuasion, until the group commenced spiritually cleansing him with noisy brutal kicks. He was dragged off by the police. Saved from further harsh confession.

Watching for the inevitable moment when the police relaxed their tight grip of prerogative on the wide eyed J. Small, Skanker saw him rush back to the company he was fighting to lunge hard, with knuckled diplomacy, into an invited warrior's face and kick an unwelcome pugilist at groin level with the glee of salvation.

"Got ya' yer bastard!"

The peeved, blue uniformed boys sprinted to sort him, taking no chances this time. Instead they handcuffed the trouble maker and allowed his combatants to walk away.

As J. Small was held tighter now, waiting to be collected by the mobile prison, one of the fighters, unnoticed by the captors, with a spleen of white vengeance, rapidly sprinted to crash hard onto the base of J. Small's neck causing him to collapse. Silently. Slowly. Obviously hurt.

His carnival was over.

Another intimidator, moving in with the slow motion of a lagered, forlorn shift worker, held a broken, jagged bottleneck to clarify a certain, ritual judgement, but was stopped, cuffed and held by alerted peace-keepers, both to wait for the wagon.

"Better call an ambulance now for him. Although he's asked for it I guess," P.C. Fund called to W.P.C. Roam holding the communicator, hoping he sounded authoritative enough.

She obediently acted, hearing this male dominance. Being young and new to the force. *Later in her career their roles are reversed. Her deputy chief constable towers over his desk sergeant.*

"He's the one!" Skanker, arm pointed at the horizontal J. Small, shouts near to P.C. Fund.

"Yes kid? What did you say? Can't you see we're busy?" P.C. Fund punctiliously replied.

Both raised their voices above ***I love you, you big dummy.***

One of the soft songs played loud to signal the end of the night disco.

"He's the one! The one who killed the bloke," Skanker insisted.

"Bugger off, will you? We don't need this! We're bloody busy!" The younger P.C. Amsterdam who acquired a bloody nose in the fighting appeared, to stand in front of P.C. Fund.

"I'm telling you! He's the one! The guy that's been knocked out. Him! There!" Skanker persisted.

"What the bloody hell is this kid talking about?" P.C. Amsterdam asked himself, knowing that the other two uniforms only spoke to him when they must, and they wouldn't know the answer to this query anyhow.

"I'm telling you he's the killer!" Skanker insisted.

"How do you know?" Proud of his contemptuous reply was P.C. Amsterdam.

"Ring up Detective Inspector Swettervil if you doubt and ask him if he knows me."

"Bollocks shitskin! Go home before you're booked. Can't you see we got problems?"

"Yeah, and I'm trying to solve one of 'em for you, you racist bastard!"

"Beg your apology I'm sure."

"Are you gonna ring him then or not?"

"OK, clever punk. If you do know him. Where do you think he will be?"

"In a boozer, of course. In 'The Stag' I would say."

Whipping round dramatically P.C. Amsterdam smiles exclamation, "Christ, you do know the old bugger then if you know that."

"I said I bloody did, didn't I?"

The ambulance arrived and J. Small, the second suspect felon of the day, was bungled in the back with well built escorts. Naturally with care. The wily adversary stayed. Chained to railings. Ignored.

And the music had stopped, so P.C. Amsterdam could converse to Skanker under less stress.

"Look, kid! We both know if it was the other way round it would be the other way round."

Skanker looks perplexed.

"You don't know what I mean?"

Perplexion continued.

"Look, if your lot ruled the world then me…er…we, the whites, us fucking palefaces would suffer right? Well wouldn't we?"

"Bollocks!"

"You fucking would, wouldn't you? I can tell by your face. I don't fuckin' believe it. You'd make sure of it."

Skanker's look says yes.

The copper relents. "All right. All right. I'll listen to you."

Skanker makes a mental note that another adult has shown maturity.

"Look, I know you're all looking for the bloke who killed the guy on the West Hill."

"How do you know?"

"I told you, because I was on the Hill and I was questioned if I'd seen any body."

"OK. So what you gotta tell us?"

"At last. You're sure now?"

"Don't get too pushy."

"Well, I think the geezer you've just put in the wagon could be the murderer."

Even P.C. Amsterdam's short experience of questioning people informed him that Skanker believed what he said and modestly admitted this to himself. He rang up D.I. Swettervil on his police cell phone and recounted the youth's story, listening attentively, being young and keen, and acted on the orders given by his superior in everything.

"Thanks, son." P.C. Amsterdam acknowledged the help of the lad. "We'll follow this up."

"Don't call me son!"

The copper's mouth twisted to squash a smile and moved away to settle a smaller afffray saying, "OK, son. Thanks."

"What did that fuckin' coon want?" asked P.C. Fund watching Skanker walk away.

"You leave that young man alone!" P.C. Amsterdam shouted back suddenly protective.

"Sorry I'm sure." P.C. Fund flabbergasted.

D.I. Swettervil's colleagues were now imbibing at the same pace as their superior, drinking and spilling beer, sitting around damp, chipped walnut tables wearing twisted cast iron legs and realising a good time when they stumble over it. The leader of the recent group drunk less than the other two as he was continuing the night's tale.

J. Small was speedily transported to the county's finest trust hospital, cautiously accompanied by the law where he was treated and wrapped partially. Taken onto the police station still drunk and unclear and interviewed, he denied everything until a jacket search revealed some horse tranquillisers in a lining.

"So what are these?" a younger fan of Fulke's enquired.

"Nothun'. They're just fo' my entertainment."

"Some entertainment!" the younger detective P. Miner spluttered, "and I think I'm dangerous with half a bottle of whisky,'" he calmly reflected.

"And this?" He held up a Smugglers Cave ticket dated the day before.

"O...Oi've nev'r seen it before," J. Small insisted slurringly when shown the date.

"This ticket," D.C.P. Miner ignored his plea, "was bought only yards from where the body was found. Now we are getting coincidental, aren't we?"

J. Small slumped forward. For the night. The policeman gave up reason.

Incoherence and bouts of sleep decreed reassessment tomorrow.

Held overnight on suspicion.

The next day the clear headed D.I. Swettervil closely questioned the accused after the routine discovery of specks of blood on his vital fluid smelling clothing fitted the same DNA group as the victim's dried interference. On being shown the evidence the prisoner asked for a solicitor and pleaded the innocence of a shoplifting werewolf.

"Oi' war' in Bex'ill. Wiv' my grandmuvver. Havin' cream tea in a tea-room on the sea-front."

Eventually persuaded by his legal aid brief to state guilty, the evidence being irrefutable, he told all.

"All is that me 'nd Ken, Ken Globun did the geezer on the 'ill but we wur' paid forrit. We didn't do it fo' fun. We're not loike that. We're straight in that way. Two blokes paid us. We wazn't sure who they were but I 'fought they were sommut to do with the carnival on account they wur' stealing carnival money. Trouble is he 'eard 'em talking about it in a boozer. The dead one. So we had to do it. The deed."

"Their names?"

"No they nev'r said. But Oi'd remember 'em if I saw 'em again. Definitely."

"Is that it?"

"Well I think they said somethin' about a power station. Maybe one of 'em lives there."

"Lock him up."

The law was jubilant having cracked the case, dancing around and nearly hugging each. As far as male bonding would allow. A sometimes back-pat. Cautious, careful congratulations to the core. Below. The taken down, locked and left J. Small carried on soliloquising. "One thing Oi didn' understand though was whoi we wur' to leave the body in that mush o' toadstools."

The police had their confession and were no longer listening.

Acoustics being too good to miss ***The clouds are full of wine (not whisky or wine)*** was tunefully sung from J. Small's cell as he looked through bars onto a sky heavy with rain.

CHAPTER SEVENTEEN

Sweat hit like a heavyweight punch.

Walking in, the prime female bodies slowly season to the pulse of humming, hothouse conditions. In-house short haired and thigh stretched, short skirted celebrate current rhythms. Their high heels paw, flirt, burn and stain the steaming dance floor under the large, sparkling, Technicolor dome of *de rigeur* deridedness.

Lights flash on the two beautiful newcomers.

Lights flashing *all their truths throughout* to dry ice mesmerising mist to piercing, lasering colours saturating hard core clubbers and Saturday night hopers searching for the true suntan of sweet, satisfying recklessness.

Blond boys more than dancing together in a knowledge others do not cross, their dreamland elsewhere *let them stay shining*; girls soaked and shimmering in today's beauty know to stare elsewhere as their interest is often in each other until awkward-limbed, dominating males compete for price and prize. Apes at rails lean on and over, cling to spin and fold out over the dance floor, loudly interrupting players in movement, until speedily sanctioned by paid muscle with a rawness frighteningly witnessed yet applauded as they are beaten, dragged and thrown through the nearest fire exit. They bounce inexpertly still feeling the world. And the concrete.

The elegant entranced duo view and squirm, somewhere below the surface.

Lengthened luminescences play and pulse in time to the pervading beat of perspiring excitement, imported or inhouse created. Hyped through to hypnotise all consciousness, the clamorous sounds meddle with the evening's drink intake, leading to the usual sensual but senseless illusions slowly becoming more difficult to decipher. Diaphoretic agents clamour for domination in an all out foaming frenzy of aromaed seduction, smells swinging to escape are routinely dampened only by the systematic applying of purchased sweet spraying aromas on the splash and replenish gogo market.

Thighs tire creating and pulsating while the pounding and lights consistently change. Bodies stay hot beginning the need to dampen sudurousstates. Throats pop the pill of fortune. Water bottles not quite priced for easy purchase.

Ballroomed bodies, embellishing limited liberty, sing, crease and binge to adulate a sweet Saturday in brief from the stagnant grief of the six day drag suspended elsewhere. Wrapped in their laudanum of physicality, perfect pose spine types stretch, perform to the rules of the night.

A moving crowd rings people insecure in outlook but safe in their hora. Some dance, some bang bottles for superiority, a girl rushes across to gossip, a boy claps to feign enjoyment, some scurry to a gossip not yet born. A see-through blouse is crowded by a hand.

The two recent, gorgeous women admire a formation group of arresting, angular skeletal females lapsing into triumphant after-burn, light-stepping a frontier stomp advertising the chase they will confidently win. As wanton satisfaction decreed by the beat, determined by the heat after the step, shift, shuffle, slide and sway of this foreplayed, meaningless happening, happiness happens. Males scurry round. All enamoured to familiar anonymity in this limited perpetuity.

Neck movement upward decries and emphasises a large screen where are, clearer seen, paid dancers clinically taunting and teasing an exploited world while showing more than tooo much.

"Feminism!" Xaviera shrugs to Sylvia as she nods to the monitors.

"Capitalism," Sylvia cynically pulsates with the rhythm.

The two women twirl the wrong generation's dance aloof and alongside the oblivious, amateur nighters who look up at the monitor to watch and study before determining how to pirouette, who to know and one foot to the other foot meaning no advance that is not a dance.

Over in a corner, DJOOKK creates animation with his clamorous, strutting muse. Too loud and proud mannerisms of perplexity. Too fast to last as patois vernacular. Spliff smoke fogs coolly to dance on turntables at height and distance. Adoration gazes from below. Successful scalers paw his domain.

Stoically jaded to the bar, full of controlled wetness and sleeping initiative, the twosome sit debruised into inconsequentials. Relief being the drink.

Similars biding the time of their lives discuss misquotes of drunkenly inspired, dicey debates at the same and other enticing but tacky bars, selling overpriced alcohol around, about and above on balconied levels, to gaze down on the co-ordinated effort and preponderant action.

Xaviera had rung Sylvia, the friend of all women, to go dancing, though why she picked that particular exercise in living she no longer remembered. Having the same publisher their relationship had faded in slowly to fade out gradually but for Xaviera's persistence, and Sylvia being pure kindness. Still here they undoubtedly are.

Anything better than nights thinking of days nearing to the time she next visits the many armed poetry editor. On her own. She knows she worries about nothing, but what can she do?

The barmaid walks the wrong side of the jump impressing as a failed starlet out of starlight but downbeat showing arrogance strained with vanity.

Sylvia notices Xaviera's small mouth dissolving into her face during demure manoeuvres.

"So why are we really here?" Sylvia looks around.

"I necded to get out of myself. That's all," Xaviera replies.

"Well I hope this has done the service," smiles Sylvia looking round.

"Some of it."

"Piss off little boy!" Sylvia snaps at a juvenile irritant wanting dance, conversation, drink or sex, but settles for failure at a safe distance.

"C'mon, let's go somewhere quieter," suggests Xaviera.

They move to a table cornered away from most mass hysteria.

Silences exist in the infrequent meetings of these two wordsmiths. During one such interlude Sylvia notices a hapless rhinoceros beetle *oryctes nasicornis* triumphantly crawling along most of the dance floor and about to reach the opposite edge, mercilessly cut down and squashed to death by stamping, Cuban heels. The death held more prominence she revised later, noticing the owner of the fashionable Spanish footwear was a lousy dancer.

"You still see Fulke in Hastings?" Xaviera thought she was enquiring absentmindedly.

"Yes. Quite regularly. In and out the pubs. Along with Malcolm," Sylvia replied as she offered Xaviera an accepted cigarette.

"A threesome of sorts then?"

"Of sorts, I guess. Though what sort I can't imagine." Sylvia made a mental note to resurrect Xaviera's memory in Fulke's mind the next time she drank with him.

"I'm not doing too well with men, Sylvia. Bloody disastrous to be true!" Xaviera declared as in failure scratching just above her left knee.

"I'm not doing men, period, Xaviera. Never again," Sylvia replied.

"I mean, I meet the most extraordinary fools, you know, you could ever hope to meet." Xaviera had not heard Sylvia's reply.

"I know. They're all out there. You can't help bumping into them," Sylvia answered. Xaviera was attentive again.

"Only last week, at an awards ceremony. Not awards for me, no. I...er...I was getting paid you see."

"Mmm." Sylvia understood the need to sustain interest.

"I met this rich tall farmer with broad shoulders, but thin long arms, good looking nevertheless. We talked nicely and agreed to meet. The next evening that is. So only two drinks into the next night's date and he is telling me that he broke someone's arm once. Now am I interested?" Xaviera stopped for a few seconds to wonder whether she was rhetorical or not. As she spoke she heard a hip hop dance version of **Dauchau Blues** and found her concentration slipping further as her mind went back to another man, time and place.

Returning she continued. "But not to look too overblown, he says. He of course did not intend to do it. Oh no. He had only walked into the local public house for a drink and was coerced into joining in the mother of all arm wrestling competitions. By now I am falling asleep. I mean how can I fall for it every time?"

"It's rather easy, you know, when most of them are of that ilk, surely."

"Oh, it does not stop there. Would that it did. No. As vanity drips from flesh he continues with his chat. It seems he watched others play until such a time as they missed a member. So naturally he joined in. Several games later he played the champion, whoever he is, and won very easily. The next day on entering the bar he was told that he had broke the champion's arm the previous night. No comeback though, he informs me. All gentlemanly, he said. I might as well be fighting off the Falbala and Fibril poetry editor as going through this. Really. It is so bloody puerile, so aggressive, so potentially possessive. When he mentioned something about Morris dancing I left. By then he'd naturally tried something physical. They don't care where they try it, do they? In front of their friends would you believe?"

"Yes, I would. That's one thing that hasn't changed. I blame it on their mothers."

"Yes, but what do you blame their mothers on?"

"Their fathers!"

They smile to titter as they watch a young woman talking and smiling at many men with her passive, male partner bending one ear to listen only at what she says to these strangers.

"Sorry, I must be boring you with all this. It's just that I get caught every time."

"That's OK, Xaviera. That's OK…Did you just say that many armed mollusc is still working at the publishers?" Sylvia chuckled.

"Yes, unfortunately," Xaviera tries to join the laughter, "and I have to see him tomorrow."

"Lucky you," laughed Sylvia loudly, now the booze is working.

So Xaviera sits in plush seating in the publisher's office, bored and temporarily relieved of attention, waiting to see the results of the week before's photo session. She has to help choose suitable pictures to place on the paperback version of her latest successful volume. The plush, racing green leather seating skirts three sides of the large room, and life's experience has told her always to sit at one extreme knowing that at the conclusion of the discussion she will be sat feverishly at the other end. Forced to move the full distance of the seating as Charles Weedon, the permanently menopausal, poetry editor of Falbala & Fibril does not respect presence but invades it.

She breaks off her health kick again by coping with a B&H donated by the hair-thinning poetry editor. Charles Weedon offers a light to her cigarette and her head moves to catch the swaying flame in his hand. He notices nothing unusual being busy gazing down at her lower limbs, admiring her thighs partly seen and partly sheen through delicate costly fabric as he thinks of the odes he writes to her. Always has and always will. Usually found in her mail to the office and never at her home. He does not overstep the privacy laws though he has been trying to lay her since litera scripta began.

Both look at the proofs. The nudging commences.

She finds the photographers interpretations of herself rather liberal, and wonders how she allowed herself to agree to so much exposure concluding that the portrayer was very pleasant and very gay which caused her to relax more than she would otherwise. Her hand feels in her handbag for a handkerchief. Charles Weedon moves away allowing her respite for the necessitated act. A touched envelope on the bottom of the bag causes her to remember being asked to post the registered letter to the poor Hastings relations who are always getting in trouble with the police that her mother had told her brother to post, and she has forgotten as well. Though if she was her parents she would have nothing to do with them, having long ago been shown strange newspaper cuttings concerning the family by her brother Rupert, who as far as she was concerned was not normal either.

Mucus membranes mellowed she returns the damp accessory to her bag. The editor is chasing her around his office again.

"This has got to stop," she thought, feeling a tear somewhere. "It's embarrassing if nothing else."

As she escapes she daydreams.

Remembering a miniature railway museum above a model shop where Fulke and she paid at the counter below to climb stairs to the exhibition above. She felt olde worlde about the place which made her think of the smell and taste of bonfire toffee when she was a girl. Not that she could mention this to Fulke, as minimally he may have sulked for hours or maximally exploded with childish contempt or merely shrugged contemptuously. Dislike of extreme emotion muted her opinion.

A partiality for diminutiveness in mechanics and electronics attracted him. She followed, only a little curious. Together they gazed and admired the large layouts of small towns and villages, contained countryside, abrupt seascape and narrow railway lines all protected by glass coverings and all at average human height with an idiot button to press to activate the transport. What wonderful things you can do with match-sticks, felt and glue, she thought, knowing he saw a different world of greater complexity.

Half hour or so passed in awe at the minutiae in the constructions when she felt his body too close for respect in a public area, and quickly looked around to notice no-one was on their storey, no cameras suspended from walls and no-one noiselessly coming up the uncovered wooden stairs. She allowed his hands to enjoy their journey over and around her hidden highs and hollows as his rail tracked urgency signalled across to her stations of desire. Carriages travelled through her countryside but his steam engined endeavours were persistently muted at tunnels. Keen ears were the guards vans and moving mouths the exhilaration of speed. Xaviera enjoyed being exploited to nationalised railways adoration until the heightened sound of hobbyist shoe to pink, painted, wooden stair instantly declared journey's end.

CHAPTER EIGHTEEN

Treblinka gleamed so ostentatiously in the terrible, brooding sunshine Fulke thought, like a brand new brazed, polished axe purchased from a Norse Gods D.I.Y. store. The car had been valeted. Naturally, as he was not going to perform the task.

Bo had asked, well she had implored him sweetly, to drive her to Udimore to see Big Rex, her poppa, play cricket for his pub team. Mockingly stricken, she had beseeched him with gifts of men's toys to please clean out the vehicle.

Now the accident maker glistened like a lit sparkler through the car glass, travelling to the desired destination, the weather looked and felt like an imminent thunderstorm, with cloud the colour of a successful mugging and warm air hanging heavy, veiled as in customised rain forest memories. The lovers observed pertinent slashes of lightning indiscriminately pierce the sky, exhibiting whimsical control over all as they drove, necessitating the both to start and the car to swerve slightly. A warmth inside informed him that he enjoyed the transport in this new finery despite his usual values, but he still had no desire to go to the imperial game and they were nearing the ground.

The Floppy Boot Stomp finished as they drove through the gates. Bo had long since accepted the cantor Captain's part in her man's life and found herself actually liking some of the songs. Just as well she had realised.

Treblinka braked to switch off. Fulke let the hand control stab the air celebrating car care.

They arrived to find the teams at tea, halfway through their carnival week annual match, blissfully ignorant of the way the wind was blowing, though an experienced sighting skyward would confirm the meteorological potential hanging near to the local derby.

Good, Fulke thought, at least we'll only be here half as long as expected.

Big Rex was playing for an Old Town boozer, 'The Lord Nelson,' that he had frequented in his wide boy youth, despite the fact he now lived out of town in affluent abundance. The pull was usual in a middle aged man. His daughter loved her father and liked to see him play. An inconvenience of emotion Fulke finds hard to take, not wanting to be around, but he amuses himself with the anticipation of rebellion these middle aged men will bestow to the world and each other.

Each team stayed with its familiars for fodder and fare, though the occasional mix spilled.

The lovers walked past the weather troubled, insufficient white paint but enough cream to cover, ground level pavilion. Fulke smelt the concentration of sweaty socks and stale clothes and realised they were passing the teams changing rooms. Checking her reflexes he understood that Bo sniffed nothing being complete focused on seeing her father and noting his health.

A group of middle aged wives, forcibly idled into catering, sat close to the portable table, interimly utensiled, rubbing sun prevention cream onto blotchy, ruffled, pink arms. Big Rex was seen tucking into a partially flattened vanilla slice accompanied by a bottle of pale ale when his daughter approached to motherly admonish him about keeping to his diet.

"Why do you think I come to the bloody cricket if I can't relax and get away from your bloody mother nagging me to eat all the bloody things I don't want to bloody eat?" He winked at her.

She listened while smiling affectionately into the eyes of his bulk.

Fulke noticed the sadly shaped sandwiches and crumbling cakes, and believed they had seen one too many changes from their original states. He wondered why others could not see the clear deterioration and stayed with the coffee even though taste here made him unsure about its pasts. No bottled beer for him as being a public figure he does not drink and drive. Especially when people are watching. This denoted that he stayed on better terms with Bo who knows he drinks too much as it is.

The tall, slim, physiotherapist friend or lover of the bearded pharmacist, part time public relations officer R. Rust, his body displaying a weakness for real ale and wearing his Jack on the green vest clearly seen through his thin, white, cotton cricket shirt over acquired rotundness, was telling him of the frustrations she encounters with male patients.

"They think I'm looking at their bodies, you know, Rufus, the bottom half of their bodies," Miss Lulu Stoops explained to the sweaty back of R. Rust who was keenly watching players practise with the ball, noticing if anyone was better than he. Fulke could quite understand why undressed men would nervously react to this long haired, bright eyed, dark beauty but he was not listening.

"How do you mean?" R. Rust turned to face her, capitulating to her call, knowing it was impossible to study people playing the game when Lulu emptied her thoughts.

"You know, down below, their private parts, always trying to hide their parts, their privates, you know, while I'm trying to do my job. Only my job. As if I'd care!"

"Oh, you mean they don't like you looking at their dicks."

"That's right! They're so conceited! Always thinking that I'm looking down there. I mean I have a job to do. I'm not obsessed. Like they are."

"Well, no. It's your job. You have it to do."

"That's so. It irritates me so."

"That's so silly, you know. So stupid. Thinking that you're always looking at their dicks. I mean what does it matter if you do look at their dicks? It doesn't matter at all. Does it?...Unless of course they've got small dicks. Then it might. Haha. Then it bloody might."

"Oh, you're just as bad. Go back to watching the others practice."

She turns to Bo to discuss men and failure and how to acquaint the two. We do not hear as R. Rust talks too loud.

"Did you hear that, Swettervil?"

"What's that?" Fulke looks over. He had heard, but being human...

The story is repeated and Fulke is expected to laugh with vigour.

He begins to fake it but is soon bored and grinds to a halt of apathy, rating himself seven out of ten on his private scale of shamming unwelcome parlance. Looking high he sees black cloud slowly drifting over to block out the sun searching for the everything dry and wonders if the teams will finish their allotted times.

'The London Trader Titans' begin to walk to the wicket. One positions each of the all to correct site as if exercising space to an exactness and economy worthy of a land sculptor. The team stand quietly awaiting the first batsman of 'The Lord Nelson' Rebels to walk out. Instead, they hear swearing and fighting from their dressing room clearly concerned with who opens the play. Minutes pass. Weather hurrying a less polite appearance. Two batsmen walk to the wicket. The fielding team wonder whether to applaud. Some do.

The umpire, sobered enough to function biasely, feigns watching. Pastel flower, summer frocked women periodically take him hot coffee in a sun prevention cream sticky mug which, being oily, occasionally slips from his hand dispelling even further his claims of sobriety.

The teams soon tense to play.

"This game was invented not far from here, you know, Swettervil. In The Weald in the sixteenth century," R. Rust brags.

"Oh..er..right," replies Fulke, thinking why doesn't the conceited shit shut up and let me watch the game. I expect he'll tell me next that Oliver Cromwell banned it.

The bowler furiously runs his straight line as if afeared that everyone will have vacated the pitch before his arrival with the pawed punishment of velocity.

Number two batsman refuses to let the speed go to waste. Ball hits wood which hooks hitglobule high.

Silly midoff catches.

Radiantly.

"Good ball!" shouts R. Rust to no-one. To Fulke, "Cromwell even banned the game you know."

"Yes, I do," Fulke found himself saying, fighting off a desire to strangle the chemist with the ostentatious, medallion sized, gold dogtag that dangled from his fat layered neck.

"But it could never disappear forever," R. Rust goes ponderously on.

Applause and despair are heard through the madding field. Polite clapping volumes slight.

Batsman walks out as batsman walks in, as Fulke walks away from R. Rust.

Batsman number three, wishing he was number eleven, asks for middle stump and waits the coming.

Happy smirking bowler applies same theory. Runs fast and throws hard object. The spheroid bounces short. The ball constant in its full toss universe.

The bowler, having foregone all responsibility of his directive, can now only watch and hope.

Behind the batsman the vertical legstump leaves the soft ground rising to fall long. The fielding team hands together. The playing team's throats and eyes curse and tighten.

Number three departs ashamed and number four, Big Rex, walks out to suppressed, vengeful applause. Most of it made by his suddenly vocal daughter. Fulke looks surprised and alarmed at the noises sounding off from the quiet, sweet, beautiful girl of demure deportment he thought he knew so very well.

A grudge match is going on here.

But no-one but Big Rex and the young fast bowler Lenny Shed know this. Apparently Lenny's dad, Larry Shed, and Big Rex worked together years before on a big scrap deal in the city, and something went badly wrong, big money style. Larry lost most of his stocks while Big Rex kept all of his and more. Larry accepted business can burn good or burn bad but his son Lenny blamed the family misfortune on the man facing him. Big Rex knows Lenny feels this way and also knows he, himself has to score many runs to save the team of his memories.

Bo stops talking clothes, men and suspension bridge assembly with Lulu to watch her dad.

Laughing confidently, young Len walks back awhile from the wicket as if the world and he are harmonious in time. Spikes perfectly dug in the scuffed up turf, he whips round to view the narrow green corridor, running to build up speed for the bodyline projectile of all globes to damage. Flying accurately down the pitch magically drawn to Big Rex's bat which dispatches the speeding, compressed cork cover point to boundary beyond undergrowth to fractious farmer's field beyond.

The coffee overdosing umpire flowers arms in confirmation of six runs as 'The Lord Nelson' Rebels tunelessly sing *'We are the Champions'*.

Lenny Shed fumes and commences his bullfighting dance towards Big Rex who again effortlessly lashes the shot to someone's heaven above securing another six runs. This time they eventually find the ball. In time for the umpire to finish a whole cup of caffeine carrying chicory.

Doldrummed loss occurs for 'The London Trader' Titans.

Wickets do not fall.

Big Rex performs like perfection of sorts. Number one batsman falls to a catch in the slips.

Number five appears snaking out to the wicket almost bumping into the umpire both aware of each other's lapsed, happy, soused state.

Lenny is back bowling a second time and facing his enemy. Walking languorously from the pitch some distance before trouncing round with finality on his visage.

Fulke, watching this bowler, does not know of his short passionate coupling with Xaviera and that she restyled and dedicated one of Fulke's earlier works to him.

The missile burned the atmosphere as it neared the mass of Big Rex who saw the spinning and heard the buzzing through the air as the weapon arrived face level. Without hesitation, white willow swung to contact forcibly with orb, which sped away low at truthful speed to loud applause, that slowly died as all started to notice the missile heading straight for silent, hypnotised R. Rust who was to be Number Seven Batsman.

And he does not move.

Laying out stomach sphericalness down, supporting head in hands, Rufus Rust is looking towards the game, transfixed by the inevitability of the shot propelling in his direction. All eyes watch the ball hit the middle of the forehead knocking him unconscious to stomach turn skyward. People rush round the slavering beard. Mouth gaping to commence erratic breathing.

The game is stopped.

"Ambulance! Ring for an ambulance!" someone shouts. Another mobiles.

Minutes later the unfortunate target comes round murmuring things unclear about women and morris dancing and being surrounded by females and jittery males. All know his mannish beliefs on morris dancing so smile nervously. Fulke is naturally helping but the lawman inside cannot really make out all the mutterings. He listens keenly.

Unconsciousness resumed and breathing calmed. A dangerous sign, but a paramedic team from a private hospital has been contacted. That is all they know.

Awakening momentarily again the injured raves feverishly, "Drug addicts…uuuummm. On the West Hill…" Quiet again. To slur, "Bastards. Where am I?" Moments silent. "Money collected...Ring of death...Bastards!" Slumps back to be carried privately.

Some folks momentarily wonder the ramblings before drifting back into their private, complex lives, but our detective stays with them. Now what the hell is he blabbing on about? Fulke puzzles as trained and as habit. And I guess I'm going to have to help him as he's a friend of the crowd, an associate of mine, too, though not one I'd pick in the usual order of things.

Soon spills of lightning, dramatically hitting an ill-starred beech tree in the next field, cause the game to be speedily reassessed followed by abandonment. Each side loudly claiming victory disputing the other team's claims by scuffles, threats and language until torrential rain pours down, from muggy firmaments, dousing all proclaimed dreams of physical superiority.

To his chagrin, Fulke, for the hundred and twenty second time, wonders whether competition is naturally inherent in mankind and reaches the only satisfying conclusion that the human animal should have been put down at the birth of his history.

All but Lulu Stoops take cover. She travels in the ambulance with her friend or lover.

CHAPTER NINETEEN

Everyone brings their pitbull look-alike on holiday. If this was true paranoia would not the dog be guarding the homestead?

For minutes Fulke watches the holidaymakers and debates their quirks refreshed by their idiosyncratic warmth. Dehydrated fish, rusty boats. People look at anything when holidaying.

He smiles as he turns to look out, towards the end of the pier on noticing boys jumping off into the sea as he with friends, years ago did before them, and others will after them.

Above, the arrogant sun competes with a fuel evaporation trail at 36,500 ft, simultaneously projecting a sordid longing for instant, sensual gratification to the influx and residents alike.

Hastings Harriers run by everything. There is obviously a marathon somewhere soon.

Is the winner already determined, depending what chromosomes were dealt each in life?

Fulke easily strides over the child fence around the miniature train patch.

"How's it going, Casey?" Impressed by the weather, he shouts happily to the short, white haired late fifties driver crouched on the too small steam engine preparing to give his young passengers a sea-front thrill or two and back. "How's business?"

"Fine Fulke, and don't call me fuckin' Casey!" Jimmy Jones replies.

"Well you're close, Jimmy! You smell like it!" Fulke smiles as he smells the mixture of salt and smoke on the wind.

"Maybe I do."

"Not so good today then, Jimmy?"

"Oh, jus' too much fucken' piss that's all."

Belgian pop music strains from the go-kart circuit, the shore situated Angling Club flies the Canadian flag, Ipswich markings seen on a boat offshore and Spanish students visit the beach.

We are nothing but vicarious.

Jimmy Jones slowly pulls away, and D.I. Swettervil, for he is working, sees, to grim but victorious pleasure, the two, ageing, emaciated to cosy, skeleton hippies with thinning hair and streaky beards, who were smashing up cars in the white crow disturbances, seated comfortably in one of Casey's carriages.

They still wear white crow on black background T shirts, under dress jackets, and are communally smoking an abundant spliff. The formidable policeman calculates how to position himself in the next carriage to the couple. He moves in subtle, slow motion so the couple do not notice him, but appearing psychotically peculiar to any objective observer. Jimmy Jones slows the units down to enable the ascension. when seated near the D.I. whispers into his transmitter to apropriates, before listening to their conversation on youth, capitalism and smashing shop windows. For life to have any kind of fairness and balance they must have had fertile fast young lives. Or claimed to have had. They frequented roughhouses once, but now the energy has gone. They play safe but give no explanation. None is explained. None is enquired.

"I saw this yellow light, man, glowing. Then a red, then a pink, psychedelic like, and I was floating man, in the room and I was only twelve man. I've never told anybody that," Tristan says.

"That's interesting, man, me too, you know. It doesn't matter what others say, you know. You saw it man, remember. I believe you. Yeah. That's an interest that is," Jake replies.

"Yeah, you know The Ridge, Stonestiles Lane? Just off it. I was with Jane, I was only nineteen, you know. Remember her?" Tristan moves on.

"Yeah, nice kid. Was anyhow. Ugly these days I should think," Jake, ageing hippie two smiles the smile of sexism. "After all, she's old now...Shit! You didn't marry her, did you?"

"No. Lucky for you I didn't, huh? And pass us that," points to the joint hanging from Jake's nicotined fingers. They both chuckle quietly, though never to be termed secretly.

Tristan, ageing hippie one, drags long at the weed and resumes.

"I'd said goodnight to her and I was walking down the lane and I saw this figure. White, blurred, misty, like shining, glowing but...I turned round and ran back. But after a minute I thought, it's not gonna beat me so I went back...and the figure had gone."

A silence occurs between the two broken by the regular clanking of wheels on metal tracks, gulls crying their epochs and carried happy children until... "I've never told anybody that, ever, I've meant to but I never have. But I saw it, man. I saw!"

"Yeah, cool interest man, cool. You know. It doesn't matter who says you did or did not see it, you know the truth. Those ordinary people. They don't believe in anything man. Anything. They don't see ghosts. You saw, man, you saw, and they don't believe in space people, aliens coming here...They don't believe in nothing. People out of their heads see more, learn about life much more than ordinary straights. Money men! Londoners! Straights!"

"I saw Jimmy too." Tristan quietly stirring to proudly peak.

"What! Morrison or Hendrix?' Jake again unsure.

'No, Jimmy Page."

"But he's not dead yet!"

"No, but I thought he was at the time!...Then I saw Hendrix. I did."

"You saw Jimmy? After he died? A lot of people saw him though, didn't they?"

"I saw Hendrix, man. Just after he died. I saw him, man. I was twenty-seven. I'd had nothing, just a bit of blow, nothing heavy. I saw him with a Buddha, 'bout this big." Shows a two foot width with his flat palmed arms moving slowly apart to this measure. "His head with this Buddha floating, for about three minutes, no words...no music ,just there, Jimmy and his Buddha hanging, then nothing, nothing. Just around...No music, man. No music at all. Life's strange 'cos I expected some."

"Lucky bastard! You know? Do you know you are? Hey! What are we stopping for?"

The train shuddered to rest to allow a determined large crowd, a Middle Earthian green politics mob to cross the track, off the beach, post their prolonged, passionate, unanimous rendezvous.

They chanted quietly, but relentlessly, to manic intensity of will.

Protect Willy! We will Protect Willy! Protect Willy! We will protect Willy!

Childish complexions of soot pierced only by the necessity of orifices coveted to the centre of the group. At the back of the procession a crescendo of frighteningly disciplined music in brass, to noise in drums and cans, to music in whistles and guitars to harmony flowed through each player and chanter.

As if the marching utopians held within themselves sufficient charm to miraculously escape the one time plague village of Eyam sterile and uncontaminated.

Indescribable, emanating power outed for obsessive beliefs to be accepted without question.

This is the reciprocal march, thought Fulke, and I'd forgotten the bloody day. They're much better behaved, but remain with the power to cause trouble. As in big.

Looking ahead, he witnessed this rough tracing of the earlier rivals, with all ages and persuasions present. Except on this run they all wear white crow cupped in caring hands T shirts and badges, and carry large colourful banners advertising these beliefs, while the woaded faces of their bairns display the same simple message: 'You are wrong! We are right!'

The omnipresent Socialist Workers Party's placards displayed 'Protect our Wildlife.'

Incredulous, remembered stares in their direction.

"They really do believe in equality then?!" Fulke hears himself.

At the initiation of the event Tristan and Jake, impacted by the power of the parade, hid cautious heads and chests into faded blue, velvet jackets, and fell swifter than their frames physically allowed between wooden, carriage seats.

Several argonauts, at the back of the somewhat dignified, funereal procession, looked mean, if meanness was needed, Fulke's experience informed him. Many of them advertised appropriate encrustations attached to their heavy maces of peace and goodwill.

The multitude of prophets continued off the pebbled beach, onto the easier trod, tarmacadam road to be satisfied with one driving lane solely, hence busy traffic could pass. Be it slower than normal. And there was a large police presence Fulke could largely see. Though three officers, unbeknown to Fulke, left the demonstration to speedily walk trainways after his call.

When the rumbling crowd eventually left, the train recommenced tracking. The two superstitious concomitants slowly rose from subduement to continue their primitive, theosophical discussion after renewed spliff intake.

"It is what's outside of you. Some people say it's all in the mind, their answer to everything, but it's what's around you, I'm convinced. You've just gotta look. That's all it takes. Like the people in this town. Some look, but most don't. When I first came here they would beat up strangers just because. Just because they were strangers." Tristan reaffirmed his philosophy.

"But I thought peace, man. I thought it was always love and peace. Especially here!" Jake interjected.

Jake thought to interject. "It is, but they beat me up; but I stood up to them. I didn't care and I fought back. Sometimes I won until I seemed accepted. I mean when they come at you what can you do?"

"Yeah, I see. Yeah. I know I suppose." Jake tries sympathy.

"Seemed though, 'cos I'd been drinking. Don't do so much now, I'm with my gods keeping fit, but when I did drink, they'd wait, leave me alone until I'd had just that little too much, then someone would sidle up to me, take the piss. They'd always be there, crack a joke, try it on, try to rile me. Many a time they'd be as good as gold, but then when I'd had just the one too many one of them would be there, or more than one, ready to make me react. To fight with them. Since my woman and child left me five years ago I've found a new life without all that. There are my gods around me and they help me. They can help you, but you gotta let them."

"Errr...I don't think. I mean I don't have the time."

"Oh they will. I was introduced to these people honest, and ones at the karate club too, all good people, no-one nasty. I thought they'd be all violent but they were all kind, not aggressive. Surprising really. I thought they'd be the opposite, and all the moves you can learn, but you only use them if you're really forced to...In about a year's time when I'll have a brown belt, near a black one, then I'll be able to walk into certain pubs and be all right because I'll be able to do something about it. Then when I get my black belt I'll be able to go anywhere. Anywhere." Tristan, ageing hippie two's voice raises slightly for this declaration. "But these other people they put me onto these gods and what they can do for me if I let them, but only if I let them. I did, too, and I've no worries. I'm helped through each day. I see them in corners, waiting to help me, smiling, at hand, to help my thoughts and whatever I try to do. I swear on my woman and child if they return...and mother's lives. These gods can make things work for me. I just have to let them and they do it. You really should try it."

"You make it sound like a new psychic deodorant, man. You know?" Jake daring to grin.

"Coming for a drink?" The interrupted mind of Fulke, quicker than instant, stops listening to look round and views Malcolm and Sylvia, cotton clothed for summer weather in tasteful pastels, smiling through colour co-ordination, yet not wrinkled or stained or splashed or torn by the night, leisurely walking slowing miniature train speed.

He need not rush to decision as the three previous lawmen approach and arrest our hippies without a whimper of clarity. Fulke watches the incoherent arrest ritual as a gleam brightens to brilliance in his dilating eye.

"Well it seems all done here, doesn't it, constable?" D.I. Swettervil reclaims confidently.

"Yes, sir," P.C. Paint replies.

"Thank you for your help." Always polite to inferiors, Fulke. He knows how hard they work.

"Thank you, sir," P.C. Calour answers.

"And I understand these, er...charming folks have some new information to give us, so I'm going to talk to them concerning that, but not here, no. Where they'll be settled comfortably...in their...er...private rooms." He points to his friends.

"Yes, sir." P.C. Paint does not believe his ears.

D.I. Swettervil departs towards the dawdling Malcolm and Sylvia. All three strategically head for 'The Lord Nelson' public house.

"Are we supposed to believe that?" P.C. Drew reinvents rhetoric.

"Well, we can't disprove it," P.C. Paint correctly assumes.

"C'mon, let's get these two anal retentives to the station, and then remind me to apply to C.I.D.! Bloody immediately!" P.C. Calour reflects emptily.

The three constables continue to enviously watch until the three friends climb the steps and disappear into the boozer. Before sighing reflectively. Consecutively.

CHAPTER TWENTY

Somebody rang and spoke. All muffled. All as usual. Most phone calls to the police station are voiced in this manner. The whole population should take cough medicine fast.

"Somebody may be there. Down at that party of sophisticates. The people you're looking for. There may be something of interest there, "a voice thinly gruffed.

"How do you know who we're looking for?" Fulke queried, not being sure himself.

The phone dialing toned after one click.

So D.I. Fulke Swettervil heads there. Dark is the night under failed street lamps.

Wearing his fashionable, summer, dark blue donkey jacket, in the pockets of which he carried his warrant card, keys, money and Fisherman's Friends, he walked down the right hand slope, the Old Town side, of the West Hill, to the cracked-paint, wooden wall door.

Honkie and rude boy bouncers stand on the door warding off everyone but the trendy.

They tried to stop D.I. Swettervil from entering as he clearly has not reached this status by barring his way. Arm of each across the door entrance.

"Have you ever heard the sound of ebony and ivory crashing at fucking speed? Have you? Ever heard one crack louder than the other? Have you now?" Fulke spoke loud, brusque and hopefully menacing. Being inches taller than both sentinels.

The commissioner agency boys momentarily perplexed, but well paid, quickly reassessed the scene and sneered. Ready to go nevertheless, they were halted by the waving of the police identity card pushed near enough to their faces to clarify no confusion.

"OK, big boy, you're in," one of them said in capitulation, hoping the policeman was not checking form in either of their backgrounds.

"Too right," said the detective.

He passed between these two clean living citizens, these doormen to the bourgeois, and commenced walking down the slope on the mortgaged side of the wall.

"But they're not in here. Whoever you're looking for," the same one calls.

"Oh, so you know, do you? In that case can you tell me what I am looking for?"

"Dunno. I fought it was about drugs."

"It usually is round here, I'll give you that, but not this time."

"Oh well, sorry. Bring us a couple of shants up will yer. If you got time?"

"Maybe. Maybe."

They hear his voice disappear as he continued moving downwards.

"And don't eat the cake!" He faintly picks up their retort accompanied by giggling.

The slope's steepness developed into a wooden staircase entering onto a long, tastefully contrived, plant-draped grotto at its base. The slant as wall was natural rock of the west hill from which was attached and constructed a large, high ceilinged, wooden veranda venturing to greenhouse, progressing onto a steep, short garden overlooking a small part of the Old Town and beach.

Reaching the ground Fulke moved along the botanical pathway, demurely passing masked partygoers, tittering and flashing expensive cameras. Into the bar area, again part arboretum, part sculpture park, part troglodytic and thankfully away from the trauma of the topiarist, he was soon recognised by a friendly barman, who despite the fact that he had many eager customers politely waiting their turn, handed Fulke a glass shouting that the beer barrels were hidden at the rear of the large crowd of smiling faces behind him. Fulke pushed through the chattering partygoers bemused that they should hold a vessel of such importance with such disregard and finding the tap in the half light he coyly filled the glass. He noted the colour of the liquid, it's always a good idea to check, and drunk it right down. The action was repeated. Somewhat initially sated, he replenished his shant and moved away from the group surrounding the butt as their stares and chuckles, it seemed to him, implied it was unusual doing what he did.

Too soon time spent watching strangers endeavour to dance with strangers and arms fetching trimmings down became a familiarity. Don't eat the cake he understood as written. Invited or not to any happening the usual fashion was a loaded cake, craftily cooked under a gleeful smile, to confuse partygoers even more than the alcohol. Sometimes the drug mix debilitated even the initiated for days. So Fulke stayed with the known drug of his choice.

Drinking and circulating with the sophistication of a truffle pig he walked out into the night air, stumbling on the uneven turf in his curiosity to edge the garden. After a satisfactory snoop and discussion about art, football and betrayal with carpetbaggers in corners, he slowly realised the whole party consisted of a group of egos that, legally or not, licked off more than their fair cut of society and imagined this acted out on every strata of government, business and entertainment.

The same minds will out and steal and I protect them. He thought a thought hidden for years.

A small, clustered group of earnest, short haired talkers and light drinkers in silk scarves, collarless shirts and moleskin jeans were somehow around him discussing the avante garde and its consequences. Gleefully he threw them a morsel of hyped hysteria.

"I fall in with cutting up livestock as a natural follow through in the British tradition of still life," he loudly remarked, waiting for vanity to reply.

"Quite. I see death as the sensational side of life, nay all existence," a suedehead answered.

"Yes, especially when it's done with a chainsaw as the tool," another long haired collar buttoned up agreed. "It brings in another dimension of dominance."

"Do you know the artist then? The one that does the creative cutting?" another pale, male face enquired aggressively to Fulke, "because if you do not, how can you criticise?"

"Well, I don't know Rembrandt. To speak to, that is, but along with others I can masturbate all night over his work. Though I guess you know the cutter, huh?" Fulke grew stronger.

"Huh..uh. Hardly. That's not really the point though, is it?" Pale male again. Stricken.

"Isn't it? It was just now. When it suited your argument," Fulke exasperates.

"The idea is the thing. Nothing else matters." Suedehead is back.

"No-one needs to draw anymore then?" Fulke pulls another string.

"That's right! Isn't it marvellous, but you do need skill." Buttoned up collar bites his hair.

"Yeah. Someone else's skill and specialisation no doubt," Fulke continues to fight for his corner.

"But the idea is paramount. The work is no good without it." Suedehead enthusiastically.

"The work is not needed with it." Pale face again.

"Exactly. Sorry I exist. Or is it you that doesn't?" Fulke turns on one or the other.

"Sorry. I didn't mean to be rude." Fake, or really upset, paleface apologises. Fulke cannot tell.

"Oh, I think I did!" He is sure.

"There're wonderful sunsets here. Don't you think so?" The pale, male, short haired antagonist, melting, appeals to the group.

"I think that nature even at its finest, at its most violent, in its apathy towards man, is just another, cultural construction within a post modernist idiom and art really does not need it," the long haired, buttoned up, white shirt mumbled decipherably dramatic.

"So Rothko painted the sunset we can see, did he?" An aside of vengeance as Fulke moves on to similar things partisan. "Or was it Pollock? After the crash?"

"Exactly, friend! You do see the argument!" Pale male jubilant.

The conversation, begun bigoted and ended flamingly fascist, finalises in Fulke's footsteps faintly heard in a distant entrance. He approaches but walks by a tall, middle aged woman, encompassing the boredom and impatience of the rich, looking up to the heavens, waiting for her small, youthful, drunken, talkative beau to pass out in order to be carried to their waiting taxi.

Perimeter passageways, leading to unknowns and toilets and private house rooms, he explored, as the inquisitive act enabled freedom to walk straight without pushing through bodies with the obligatory sorry dropping from the larynx. With this rite exhausted and nothing to attract his mordant curiosity, the decision to drink another beer before the off was made. This time round the casks were still smothered solid by a crowd. It was only with prior knowledge he knew the position. The partygoers, on seeing Fulke politely make his way through them and help himself to a beer, considered this one of the most hilarious acts committed since the deification of saints. Fulke was bemused to the point of embarrassment by their reaction. "All this noise and laughter and all I'm doing is getting a drink. Am I properly dressed? Look down quickly. What do they do for a hobby? Maybe they snort something different as a diversion off the norm, but they need to be high on something to find my drinking a shant amusing. Maybe I've a new growth somewhere I don't know about. Or maybe they've had some cake," he pondered aloud to himself.

A safe DJ played appropriate music to the crowd and its moods, and the hour for well known folk ditties was floating loudly through his head when someone spoke to his ear. "That's the area to look in," the nasal voice said. "Jingerly jangerly land."

He turned round lazily, but of course the voice had disappeared into the mass of arrogance and false happiness. Now if that had been a woman's voice I'd have moved quicker he surmised.

Voices. The age strained couple return.

"You view a god on the television and you notice the hair, its awayness, above the left ear, above all the built up bouffant, hair sticks out loud and free. Why always in that place? Why always at an important time? Eugenically happened or merely accidental but always it remains?" Adolescent to middle aged.

"He borrowed everyone else's songs, you drunken shit." The older female voice articulating to her maudlin shaver of a boyfriend.

"Who did?" the younger male voice slurs.

She was still tensing to go.

"Elvis did," the older female replies.

"Sideburns boy," her juvenile male adds, "That hair stands unfortunately embarrassed without you knowing. Or me too…Let's go…Shall we? Home to bed?"

"OK." She giggles as if it was his proposal.

Their taxi driver is relieved, preferring work to nicotine smoked thought.

Masked faces relentlessly continue sated searches for drink while refining poses, hoping to find someone to tell them fresh dreams in this hollow in the West Hill. All guarding illusions preventing anyone to enter in their dream of a happiness distinguished in vapours. Many varieties hung in the air held by what to do and why. Just breath in. As he walked through a mask spoke, "I am part of this, am all of this and I dwell between realities."

"Of course you are! Well, don't let me interrupt! You style pile of detritus demented dimensions!" He thought he had replied very well.

Despite the late hour the enclosed, glass, husbandry entrance was full of failure, duplication and aromas. Enough of the blowheads, he turned to walk back under cover towards the chalk West hillside, onto a long, caved corridor that he now knew suggested the approximate area of the toilets. On stepping inside he found a noisy throng, still going strong, of excitement, desperateness and alcohol littering the floor which slowed his intention.

After consequential success he strolled out. Contemplating a left move through the crowd there was mumbling behind, near his left ear, for a second time tonight.

"Fairies! Dancing fairies you want!" The voice whiningly, whispered redemption.

"Who…?"

He turned but no-one was near.

A figure, frantically pushing through the partygoers in a blue and white bomber jacket and a misshapen paunch, caught his eye. Was that him? Not because he was sure this was the intimate speaker, but because that kind of dress was unexpected at this type of upmarket venue.

"Who was that slapper you were speaking to, Fulke? That mush carried a parapluie paunch all right," one public-spirited piss artist spoke.

"I…I.." An attempt at replying passed through the detective's mind.

"Johnny Bitter. Johnny Wayne Bitter. Fucking religious nut. The son of…Cain Humen, you know…the pervert," another imbiber interrupted to proclaim. "Who let him in? Not the type of place to see a person like that unless he's turned over an old leaf, but then it's not even autumn."

CHAPTER TWENTY ONE

Fulke sat momentarily straight-spined before comfortably slumping forward.

Once relaxed, he began to brood on the bland expectations of the coming evening leaning on this polished, South American hardwood jump, in a recently-renamed, off limits, rough boozer. Stuck somewhere geographically recessive the welcome walk-in insistently feigns to be a winebar in an upmarket area, but protrudes on the purlieu of downsizing streets.

The ceiling is stained with the gloom and glamour of a million nicotined nights; a television in one recess shows young, female singers chanting of an unnamed, individual freedom yet dancing in tight accord; on one wall hangs a framed, pencil drawing of the young, rock'n'roll, piano player Jerry Lee Lewis sat in the cockpit of a Second World War, American Harvard warplane; while a large, ex railway station clock close states the clamour of everyone.

Below these collected and valued objets d'art stand, sprawl and sit prune wrinkled, once white bodies discussing the number of DHS claimants they can squeeze into their individual properties, how the socialists are ruining the country whether they are in power or not, and does anyone think their leather trousers are too outrageously daring to wear. Or are they really leather jeans? *They have been known to squeak.*

"A boozer called a wine bar they call a fucking wine cellar! Imagine meeting the love of your life in one of these places. I hope no-one sees me here," he muttered to no-one looking around, gulping down more of his beer. "There's real boozers up this same street too. Why couldn't we meet there? Oh no! Not fuckin' good enough! We have to meet here, and then we're going to a restaurant. A fucking tapas bar, for god's sake. I'll never live this down!"

He had lost and knew it.

The folk duo staged behind him had presence. Melody as manic monolith. They strummed their stringed weapons of anguish and protest demanding things intangible from their audience, but receiving rude dismay within murmuring mass apathy from the part time spectators gathered. The musical pair loudly drained lost emotion out through walls and from the sitters, to generally downgrade the taste of the beer. Passions were forced out front doors and emergency exits to randomly headbutt the psyche of humanity cowering somewhere inside or out the neon-lit building. Though no-one ventured any criticism as no-one cared.

One of the pair wore a hard crazed look contrasting with his bulk of soft, black, long, curly hair signifying, the two women in his life that should never meet were both in this bar, and were talking to each other quietly and gazing towards him from time to time. The other unimpressed, ceiling tall, red haired and bearded instrumentalist laid back and dreamt of cocaine and country music in either order.

Along the bar.

"What's that he's playing?" Man to woman.

"I've never seen one before." Woman to man.

"No. What's that he's playing?" Man.

"I told you. I've not seen one before." Woman.

"No. What is that he is playing?" Man irritated.

"I don't know, but it's got strings on it and it plays music." Woman.

"What?"

"I don't know, but it's got strings on it and it plays music."

Seconds later.

"Do you want a fuckin' broken nose?"

She stayed quiet but several of her seconds later was seen to grin out of his vision.

Another happy couple.

The complacent crowd stayed with their thoughts layered in nazis in Poland, alien abductions in Wales, crying statues or faith healings that happen. Fulke was compulsively reading their thoughts as there was nothing better to do, until he noticed Bo's head and shoulders peering through one of the porthole doors and a pleasant recollection of the afternoon developed as he remembered her cleaning of Treblinka. Pink all over in tightness, she stretched strategically over and around the motor car, washing as she did so, to become damp in places as splashes of soap and water untidily fell on her. It had been a warm day, clear and hot, but not too close and the vehicle dried quickly. When Bo had concluded the job she swore to never attempt and stepped back to admire her endeavours, she noticed her wet stained clothing. She gently scolded Fulke for not making her aware of this while he stayed confused as to why stretched clothing around her pelvis area should excite him so. He shrugged his satisfied shoulders saying something like, "If I'd have told you you had a wet minge you may not have finished the job, and I wasn't going to do it."

She hung her head partly astonished.

"And anyway I enjoyed watching you."

She slowly smiled triumphantly.

Present thoughts returned as he watched her pensively walk away from the building approximately heading back towards her transport. Two steps forward, one step looking behind.

"Here we go again," he smiled.

Calico framed portraits of dead dogs hung on the jump walls lit from above plus 'I love Salukis' in coloured lights around the glass of one particularly large frame.

Long dead dogs still stare, he thought, though they're not thinking, but at least they're not playing snooker.

The folk duo reached the culminating and loudly emphasised, heart tugging, warbled line 'The land of the dancing dead' and all around everyone agreed the appropriateness of the line.

The conversation at the nearest table became as haunting as a lost swab.

Large shouldered and large thighed with flesh to consolidate the frame, mouthed to megaphonic, the plump, middle aged woman's voice irritated the surroundings. "Well, I'm eating. Do you want anything?"

"What?" A skinny, shriven, shifty, middle aged man's voice.

"I'm hungry. I'm gonna get something to eat."

"I'm all right."

"Well don't moan later because I'm not cooking tonight."

"All right."

"So do you want anything?"

"I dunno. Where are you getting it from?"

"I'm getting a take-away."

"So you're getting a take-away. Congratulations. I didn't ask you how it was being served you, did I? I said where were you getting it from?"

"Don't fuckin' start. I'm not in the mood. I've been working bloody hard while you've been sat on your arse drinking."

"I've been sorting fish."

"I bet that's hard work, and takes all day."

"What are you having?"

"I'm having an Indian."

"Huh?"

"I thought I'd have an Indian for a change as I've been working hard and I'm very, very tired.

"Oh, are you?"

"Yes, I am. So?"

"So? What do you mean, so? So?"

"Look! Do you want any fetching or don't ya?"

"Yes. If it's OK."

"What do you mean if it's OK? Of course it's fucking OK or people wouldn't eat it."

"Well, I mean…. I mean I don't want anything that looks like babyshit."

"What? It looks all right. It always looks all right. You're always sniffing around for some of mine when I just get the one."

"Oh, I don't know."

"Well what would you want if I was cooking?"

"Are you going to cook then?"

"No I'm bloody not. I'm only asking you what would you want."

"What's the point in me saying then, if you're not bloody cooking the stuff?"

"OK, OK, OK. I'll bloody cook then."

"You will?"

"I will."

"I don't believe you."

"I will, I will."

"Yeah?"

"Yes."

"OK, then. I'd like something nice and tasty and traditional."

"Like what?"

"What?"

"Like what?"

"Well something simple and nice like, er, like Shepherd's pie."

"You're a laugh a fucking minute you are." She chuckles in contempt.

"What do you mean?"

"Nothing. Absolutely fucking nothing. Ejaculate mate."

"Huh?"

"Wank on. Go on."

His dampened demeanour, debilitated to defeat, remained in confusion. He had forgotten one basic male maxim. Never live with a woman you cannot arm wrestle.

And still Bo was hanging near or around the door wondering whether or not to enter. He liked this about her, though occasion for irritation roamed here. Having finally noticed Fulke's presence, Bo made her summer print, so short, shift dress move, to not quite stumble through the bar entrance in self conscious unfamiliarity to the situation. Eventually reaching his sprawling frame across the bar and greet him wisely.

"Fulke," Miss Bo Priscilla Viall uttered.

She always greeted him with the one syllable. Never hello or open a wound or it's pissing it down out there. Just the one name, and then a silence until he speaks. Maybe she's thinking something. Thinking what? he wondered.

The top half of her head moved at a different speed to the bottom half. He had noticed this fascinating physicality soon after their initial flush had stabilised. From the nose up her excited features appeared like two hoverbirds in dispute over ambrosial pollen while the bottom half of her countenance spoke measured and solemn in a slow motion frame contrast. She walks with a wiggle but her face does tricks he secretly announced.

"Bo," he acknowledged through sloth and not to mock, "So how was tonight's high impact aerobics lesson then?" Noticing on crossing her legs how her right thigh widened out onto the firmness of the left.

"Oh, OK I suppose."

There was a strange, wild attraction exhibited here that strained and curtailed his emotions.

Why did I ever bother with a fucking hippie?, he thought, we meet to talk of our relationship, the one she already knows and all we both hear is the hippie shit that she'll speak and hear.

Bo begins their conversation.

Fulke hangs on thoughts of the wondrous image of the horizontal dolichocephalic, blinding gleam of reflected sunlight on the polished chrome of hundreds of motorbikes outside The Esplanade drinking palace 'The Carlisle' seen from the beach off duty, off discipline, off cutbacks, on drink, on a Bank Holiday weekend. How the mundane can become sublime.

"A controversy," she mentioned.

A controversy? And I've only had two pints, he thought, finding himself listening.

"Excitement, Fulke. The past. Our past. To do with a bypass I read. Apparently King Harold in his 1066 landing landed somewhere else. He landed at Bulverhythe and not Pevensey Bay."

"Well, my first thought is we get a revisionist historian in here, as any National Front historian could have a lot to do with this, but apparently no. It's not that interesting."

"No!" she interceded triumphantly. "It's merely a charming wheeze to procure a national, cultural and historical, treasure centre instead of a three lane motorway at the back of town in all its beauty. Everyone agrees apparently. The people have chosen."

"That's...what...I...was...going...to...say!" he frustratingly, slowly echoed.

Seeing friends he nodded, not saying hello as his mind is hooked onto hers. By ignoring the room and its players he finds quiet enjoyment in their intimacy. Slumped over a bar and Bo he felt confident and dangerous, never wondering how their familiar chats sounded to her. She invariably forgave his tactile, saturnalian state, taking all she needed from these occasions.

Some one from out of town asked the barman for his creamiest beer.

"Beer or lager?"

The male world looked up to view this sad vision of the English School of Bar Apprenticeship.

Quietly Bo continued, "Do you think other religions, you know like white magic, British knights errant, etc. are getting a strong hold in some people's consciousness because there's a lack of involvement in traditional temples, with their complacency and their age old customs, Fulke? Especially near the millennium?"

Fulke sighed long and deep before deinking another pint of enchantment without replying, as he now believed in videoed cosmetic surgery and glueing buthchers' names on a bouncy castle as art. Such conceptualism of manners!

"Just be my succubus for the night?" he pleaded, still dwelling on how much damage Marcel Duchamp had done to modern art and all because he couldn't draw!

She looked down at his two button open necked, light blue shirt watching reddish brown hair struggle to leave his chest and smiled knowing others will think Fulke's black head hair is dyed.

"Again?"

"Again!"

"Of course."

Tender, silent moments in which gentle smiles collide.

"So exactly where are we meeting them?" Fulke wanting to get this foolishly arranged rendezvous out of the way quicker than now.

"In Harris' restaurant. Any minute now," Bo replied, "so drink up."

"Where's that?"

"Old Town. On High Street. Near the bottom."

"Your brother coming, is he?"

"No. You don't get on you two, do you?"

"It's not my fault. I was just trying to make friends. You told me he was in a rave band, so I merely asked him what instrument he played. He said switches. So I left it at that."

"He's only seventeen, you know."

"Old enough to annoy me."

"So what's new?"

Fulke was sitting on the same level as everyone else. Something he wasn't used to. Usually he looked down on his customers, but tonight... How to judge and act became the problem, having no experience of sitting and having a meal with Bo's parents, Big Rex and Bunny, they being two of the party. The late, middle aged couple had been nice enough to him so far, especially after the realisation that he can do anything with their prodigious dog, the only person that can control it. The older couple were not a contest, but then nobody was.

This was a celebratory dinner, a family affair plus guests, for which he was not thankful, though he knew on these occasions how some dive to depravity in slinging food and slashing souls. Apparently this lot would not rock any boat, aboard or not. He told himself it would be superior to the vegetable samosa and black pudding left, hygienically covered, in his flat.

The first course kicked in with the violence of an industrial stoppage. Long silences between swallows, gulps and mastications were spotted. Voices did not open, hence his quasi drunken tones finally, coaxingly spilled out the one and only French joke he knew concerning Belgian females and their bodies. Instantly the situation seemed bad. Until as one, spluttering laughter, giggles, and mirth mixed with relief and flight from boredom rose from the partially full mouths of the diners. A realisation of conceit settled through his frame from the realisation that he could be the master of ceremonies for the night. Even Bo's parents tacitly inferred him carte blanche on what to do and how to do it in their obvious mime.

This surprising revelation caused him to drink another large glass of wine at an increased speed, causing breathless coughing as something went 'down the wrong way'. Maybe it was that last piece of chicken he coughed, when everyone around knew all food obviously went down the right way while liquids of sin decided different.

Throat cleared, the meal went on.

Fulke found himself developing a drunken, piss-taking rapport with one Peter Gullhanger wearing the corduroy and cheesecloth artist garb of the failed augur, another momentary soulmate, but usually too cosmic in blow, to know language is a communicative process.

Life and meal had to go on and did.

The four older partygoers Bo's parents brought along from next door ate and spoke nothing to the younger elements and even less to each other. Bo assured Fulke this was how it was done. Others spilled out scatological, sexual and racist scathes intermittent with belches, burps, sneezes and positive compliments on the vittles they rampantly consumed in and out of mouth, table, napkin and floor. She held her own; he was grateful for that as he felt tested.

Any line thrown at him and his potentially aggressive reply was dampened by her belated after line positively strewn across any negative emotions. But then he always needed some help. Occasionally he admitted it.

Intermittently leaving the dining table for a drink at the bar with friends and unbelievably receiving no nasty looks from her parents warmed his frame.

In fact it seemed like he could do no wrong in their eyes. Jesus, I wish I knew what I know, he shouted inside. Later he would have time to explore the theme.

But he won't.

CHAPTER TWENTY TWO

He found out where she lived from simple detection work.

Looking at the publicity irrelevancies on the glossy paperback cover of her last publication gave him all the information he needed. Simply mobiling the publisher to mention the old friend angle would coax it out of them. Especially once they had informed her he wanted to get in touch. He felt certain that she would want to see him.

He was right.

Falbala & Fibril called him back the very next day with her address and phone number.

His call was weeks ago.

Another voice had answered the phone and surprised him to rearrange his speech.

"Miss Hume, please. Xaviera Hume. I believe she resides there?"

"That is correct. Miss Hume does reside here."

"Could you put me through to her do you think?... It is within your capabilities? Is it not?"

"I'll try and put you through. I'm only the warden you see." The voice clearly stating belief in its own supremacy.

Yes, you're only the warden, Fulke thought, only.

"Thank you, I would like that."

"What name should I say?"

Fulke informed this failed tyrant.

"Could you wait a moment?" the ageing, crackly, military, male voice enquired.

"Yes...Thank you," Fulke replied, wondering what else he would do with a phone in his hand.

Half a minute passed.

Xaviera was reclined, watching contrived, compulsive, crass television, noticing how the programmes seemed dull and uninteresting while the advertisements glowed with turbocharged relish and compulsive vibrancy when the doorman rang.

Irritated by this unwelcome interruption to her regular research she snapped back.

"What is it?"

"There's a call for you Miss Hume." Empire arrogance speaks clear.

"Who is it?' She rasped anticipating some literary groupie wasting her valuable time.

'It's a Detective Inspector Fulke Swettervil," emphasised the ex serviceman porter with a patriotic seriousness that stated this is no English name.

"Put him through will you, please?" She hoped he would not notice the tremor in her voice and interpret it as a guilt rather than nervousness.

"Right away, miss."

"Hello," he said to Fulke.

"Yes."

"You're through now," the stiff, objective voice implying that I may be talking to you though I'm sure you're not British.

"Thank you."

"Hello?" Another voice. Her voice.

"Hello," Fulke said again and wondered on parallels.

"Hello...Where are you?"

"What do you mean? Where am I."

"So it is you, isn't it?...Where are you?" He heard her husky, emulous breathlessness as realisation dawned less than immediate.

She still sounds as good as he remembered. He remembered.

"I'm on the phone. Trying to talk to you. In a boozer."

"Now that's a real surprise. Where is this...er...boozer?" He could tell her voice was smiling.

"In my still favourite town."

"Oh god! Still over there?" enthusing curiosity..

"Naturally."

"Why aren't you here?"

"What do you mean, why aren't I there?"

"Well, I just thought you might be playing as you did, you know, and you're actually around the corner like you've done before," spoken slowly and persuasively.

"What, just like that? After all this time? Please. You must be thinking of someone else. Not me."

She remains silent. He accepts the line failed and talks on.

"I was supposed to know if we could get together first, wouldn't you say? Before any of that?"

"You know we can."

"I do?"

"You do."

"So we can?"

"We can."

"That's it then."

"Why the silence?" she eventually enquires.

"Why not?"

"So you're coming?"

"I'm coming."

Hence Fulke found himself driving along Kingsway on Brighton sea-front looking for a particular sepulchral block of flats he learnt to recognise, as ***Trust Us*** liberating melody through the car speakers temporarily deafened a young cobweb spider, *Tegenaria gigantea,* practising an early, orb web behind one of the backseat spiel boxes.

The building looked rich, guarded, divisive and exhibited a tacit acknowledgement that all is not equal. A portentous supremacy shiftily shown rather than proudly displayed, except of course in the tasteful, mock, crenellated roof edging.

It was early evening and the rush hour traffic was at last beginning to thin out. He had sucked three 'Fisherman's Friends' driving here. The miasma was winning and Fulke knew he had to breathe away from Treblinka. For the time of day and the type of town and on the seaside of the throughway he parked, unusually easy, preferring not to search for the tower's underground car park, not knowing the block so well.

This block of recompense.

He left Treblinka calmed and locked.

The flat, tranquil sea was giving off little promise of anything. The sky exhibited the colourful sunset stolen from many a department store painting, but without the sparsely donned, dusky maidens, macaws and German Shepherd dogs in the foreground. As he walked over to the brooding monolith and began to climb its welcoming, concrete steps, his experienced eye noticed a few of the many black rubbish sacks to the left side of the building expertly pecked. Presumably the ones with rich pickings. Neck craning, his gaze sought the top of the building to notice far off flying feathers soaring, mostly seagulls, those proud birds he felt for, flying in and away. He thought again of Chekov, his departed, pet bird.

Knowing that Xaviera had naturally leased a penthouse pad, her image you see, and gas central heating here he hoped, a plan of calculated, eventual cleverness was evolving inside. His steps hit with disparate emotional statements until eventually reaching the precise height for a finger to press the janitor button.

At that moment he caught the sound of an ice-cream van's chimes in the faint distance caustically playing a refrain from '***The Ride of the Valkries***' while it proudly sold overpriced ices to the unlucky and unemployed on a nearby council estate.

Inside.

She still looked as good as he remembered her. He remembered.

Well, from a distance. Though, on closer inspection there were lines, not always where they were, if they were there at all.

The skin colour, cream to white porcelain, suffered sprinkled, occasional, tessellated freckles seeming to fall as a waterfall stream pouring seductively over parts of the body, while still more sweetly beguine pointedly emphatic at the limb joints. A sweet bacchanalia of dots. Another rash of spots before his gleaming eyes.

The seemingly still small waist and flat stomach as before, that must have been hard work, under the camel coloured angora dress tighter than skin. Tiny, copper curls still fell to shoulders and beyond. Delicate gold filigree around her wrists and one ankle. Colour co-ordinated, naturally. Her wide eyes remained with their haunted look, black eyeliner to perfection and surrounded by delicate, smudged, pastel nuances rainbowed to seductive effect, but with too much lamplight sparkling in them suggesting contact lensed vision. The always sweet, sensual, soft, pastel coloured lipstick, swell lipped mouth never haunted with halitosic aromas.

Her 'you can have me anytime' attitude had changed to 'take me with style, wit, decorum, sophistication and a clean change of underwear within my sub culture only,' and her pretty neck birthmark had only ravaged to a map of Ulster without the violence.

When they made love. This time like last time. Like their first time?

At the point of time *l'affaire de con* commenced she enticingly murmured, "Welcome home!"

I do not wish to claim that privilege, he thought to himself with a sudden realisation that maybe she is not what she claims to be, but then she does not claim to be anything apart from a successful poet. So maybe transmitted AIDS could be his tortoise shell to termination.

Whatever it is, it is too late now, he knew.

Being in between men as she was, though not as closely in between as she would like, she judged him on her code and on his/their past and found him worth a lengthy flirtation.

Steady money with looks that show he does not look in a mirror too often, though obviously thinks he is Billy Fury, still handsome, perfect platysma on a continuing healthy, beautiful, compact body to perform satisfyingly, sensuality accompanied with a lively though sexist mind and agreeable, lenitively ludic conversation. In his middle yeared, straight nosed, pale, world weary, squarish face displaying thickening eyebrows at war, she could see the boy that had been and the old man that would be endow his being with a warm, surrounding radiance she found cute and maternal.

Where he had always towered around and above her, an act she absorbed as projected protection making her feel less naked to the world. The need to internalise a lover was his only way of existing in any relationship. Something he would readily admit to anonymous, male bonding boozers but never to the woman.

And for this replicating time in their continuing relationship, to known realisation inside, he found himself manipulating present thought.

Be it a different intensity.

Still, this had to be done. On both sides.

She sat, thoroughly organised, with a coloured pencil in hand and notepad at the ready, being at that particular stage of being a soidisant, literary celebrity. Not really wanting to miss anything either of them said if it had the slightest future relevance to fame and money, she sharpened again the already acute B lead to an even more pernicious point with her plastic Landseer reclining lion pencil sharpener. A precursor of fashion. A cultural bargain she could not resist one day in 'The Lanes'.

Brighthelmstone's shopping mall answer to moneyed culture in a one-upmanship society. These alleyways of extortion, these jennels of genuflection, these twitters of tautology were fabricated full of illusions for people like her.

She held a cigarette when a hand was free. Her asthma inhaler in its purple lurex wrap sat coffee tabled nearby next to her chloroform choking carboy crammed with dying plants.

On one wall hung a large, framed reproduction of a Max Beckmann torture scene, interior crowded to burst with tormentors and their persecuted.

Noticing her veined hands advertising the truth of age stained in sun-bronze dye, Fulke knows no-one escapes there. Looking seriously in her direction he saw a disbelief. She seemed to have been crying, or was it just another fake? Surely she wouldn't risk all those facial gestures out of control now?

He had seen this paroxysm of movement before. When she had wanted her way.

And he had wanted his.

Her face had turned to blubber and back to sad beauty through to helplessness. Nerves and muscles had created new programmes of form, witnessed as superficial movements of the visage, to surprise the viewer with their variety and caricature. The top lip covering the bottom one thinning out the sensuality as the eyes cried out for attention.

No, she wouldn't risk that at this stage. Or would she? I've got it. She's a lonely one. Though why? At her stage of the game you'd think... but then, what price status? I'm a fool for that approach she knows it. Faked or not.

Fuck it. I'm going to be nice.

CHAPTER TWENTY THREE

"Still smoking then?" he queried, noticing specks of cigarette ash land on the expensive kilim.

Embarrassment made him move out of the air filled, see-through armchair onto the floor. He thought he would have sat there much longer, but no.

"Not really. These aren't smoking," she smiled a reply. In her voice still the quite desperation.

"No, of course not." Supercilious male retort.

"No, they're Superking 'Lights'. I'm on a health drive."

"Of course you are."

"Just because you managed to stop."

"I did, didn't I?"

"Superior!"

"Yes!"

A weekend, colour magazine, contrived to be opened on the art page laying on the divinely polished, deal floor, caused Fulke to utterances.

"Because a being has a compulsion to go out and carve or model five hundred, life-size figures with the stoic, fatalistic looks of every man, and that's usually because he can't sculpt any other emotion on the faces, so the faces have to stay that way; because he, or she, does this and spreads them over a large area, say two or three fields. The action does not make him clever or smart. It does not mean he should be greeted as a bloody genius. Or even as an artist. Doing a thing like that doesn't mean you're automatically very clever. We could all be famous if that was the case. After all, he could be just a lost soul desperate for human contact. He could be a lost wandering psychotic. He could be psychologically desperate for family life. Or worse, an inadequate that likes cities."

Fulke had noticed the main article and Xaviera smiled contentedly on hearing his harmless rant. Everything suddenly seemed as the long time before.

A silence descended like domestic comfort. Both felt the sensation and were pleasantly surprised this state of being between them had survived. He was shocked to realise he could get used to this way of being and consequently felt awkward.

She quietly enquired, "What linguist idiom does one need to write in if one's work is to be understood in twenty years time?"

"Jesus, woman. You think you're that good?" Surprised at her ambition.

"No, it's just…I wondered. That's all right, isn't it?"

"Mmmmm. I guess."

"So what do you think?"

"Well, it would surely have to appeal to the masses, wouldn't you say? They are the ones to buy the work after all! One sure way to do that is to adopt some mid-Atlantic slang, as the colonies is where language development is coming from these days, I suppose, and at speed." He was getting onto his pulpit. "At least until the Hispanics take over, but that won't happen without a bloody big fight."

"You still doing a bit?" Xaviera asked caringly.

"I'm still doing a bit, and I'm feeling hungry," cheeky fucker, he thought, as he replied.

"No, tell me what you think. Please," she implored.

"Well, again, writing has become like everything else, hasn't it?"

"Has it?" She tries not to look quizzical.

"Yes. You see, before big money became embroiled in literature all work was judged on merit, but now if it sells it suffices. So you get a new young wonderful author who can do no wrong until two years later when the next new wonder boy or girl appears, and suddenly the first scribe is fighting for a living, and after being used to big money, but that's only my opinion. Others would no doubt disagree and show evidence to counteract this," he expounded.

"Oh, I see. In that case I must be doing pretty well then?"

"As it happens. Yes, you are." Hopes his voice does not betray him.

"And I'm doing women's reading groups."

"Good for you. They're a strange phenomenon too."

"You're only saying that because they're women."

"No, I'm not. I admit I do sometimes, but not this time. Males do this as well, you see."

"Thank you for that anyway." She smiled suggestively at him as physical appreciation.

"That's OK," he not knowing if he was pleased or not.

"But I don't know how long it's going to last?"

"No, you don't, but then nobody else does either. Other dangers like using words until they lose their original force, a kind of inflation takes place. Sensational words lose their power. A style is a fashion until people tire and so on. A Dostoevskian future society favouring mediocrity and destroying genius occurs," he believed.

"Now you're confusing me...Or you're talking shit. How can you guarantee change so quick?"

"It's no shit. I wouldn't do that. You can't guarantee it, but that doesn't mean it won't happen!"

Xaviera's mind shrugs her shoulders as she decides to give up on this dialogue.

Smiling he moves to her 'fridge, and, opening it, notices vegetarian bacon in sealed see-through plastic film, reminiscent of pop art sculpture in its grandiose simplifications, sparkling in the icebox light and looking like something listeria seeking vampires nibble on between meals or on the altar buffet at a moonlight mass of virginal violence.

"Don't touch the midnight blue quartz crystal in there, Fulke, please. It needs to remain pointing in the direction it is facing until the first evening of the winter solstice," she implored with the disingenuous passion of a defrocked television evangelist.

"I won't." She's getting worse, he thought. "I'm only hungry. I don't want a cure for water retention. Or any other retention come to think of it. I'm into full flow you know."

"Mmmmmm, I know you are." She giggles a changed mood.

Me and my mouth he thought.

Nothing fancied here he quickly realised, trying to look behind the cottage cheese and celery for some glaciated but solid inspiration. "I should have known," he muttered.

"Fancy going out for something?" he innocently enquired.

"You and your decaying flesh," she smiled out at his meat eating habits.

"You and your hippie shit," he leered back at her vegetarianism.

"I'll send out for something. I know what you like. You haven't changed so much surely?"

"I haven't changed at all." He knew.

"Meaning?"

"Oh, nothing. Nothing at all." Everyone a starter. He foolishly forgot.

She makes a teasing phone call to a take-away she obviously knows well, and returns to them.

"You cook now?" she queried honestly.

"A little."

"Strange. You used to say that water didn't boil properly."

"Well that water bloody didn't!"

"But it does now?" Xaviera trying hard not to patronise.

"It had to."

"No it did not!" she mocked adamantly.

A silence from him.

"So how should my work go? You have read some, I presume. Tell me!" Xaviera implored coquettishly.

"Do we have to start this one again, as we seem to be getting on so well this time?"

"I don't know what you mean," she flustered.

"I'll remind you then. I celebrate genius and trash! Genius and trash with nothing in between! Not a society of mediocrity with genius squashed at its every birth!"

"You're repeating yourself now. You and your recondite perfection or nothing."

"That's right! No indulgence in the superficial! I told you! If you can't stand the heat of the ink stay off the damn manuscript." A simplistic ideology echoed.

"But on my terms?" She tried to steer him back.

"What about your terms?"

"So you won't take me seriously then?"

"I will if you wish it."

"But it's serious according to your terms isn't it?"

"So it would seem."

"You talk with conceit." Xaviera sees things that way.

"I may personify the arrogance of man, but never his vanity."

"Then you're jealous, aren't you?" she said slowly, realising she may have gone too far.

He did not answer. Instead, he gave her a look carrying a heavy weight of patronising violence she had never witnessed before. She heard the well timed knock at the door break the mood and moved more than quickly to collect their repast.

The meal was soon shared out to selfish appropriateness on a nearby raw wood table. He receiving the largest share, and the dual digesting commenced, their recent silence forgotten.

Both ate with polite, conversationless gaps through initially sometimes noisy, embarrassing mouthfuls, swallows and gulps neither having eaten, accompanied in this take-away style, for such a long while.

Confidence, once begun, soared, as is its genetic force, and tumbled into technicolor juices running down chins as fun begins. Coloured sauces scarfed to mouth slowly slobbered onto flesh gradually accompanied by smiles from the one and pouts from the other.

A spell fell.

All around the two.

Each looked at the other. Eyes sparkled. Mouths smiled to grin. Bodies began.

Both became aware of repeating a familiar formula. Physiques relaxing with celerity slipped down and round both carvers. Their seats slipping below their seating nearer to the floor. Still the food kept meeting the mouth accelerating steadily with the chewing unashamedly louder as the game metamorphosed. Open-mouthed munching in evidence and unwanted, uneatable, unpleasant looking residue carelessly liberated to the carefully coutured, carpeted floor behind. This was becoming familiar to many another, similar traced, eating scene. Other juices were joining the melange. Shoulders shrugged and accepted the physical inevitable.

Salivas mingled. To touch in some romance.

As it was written. To always be revised.

The food was forgotten. The meal was never finished.

The copyright of the concept safely held.

Geographic conduct became bountifully bedchambered.

An unignorable, all embracing, sensual, total sweetness heightening to a mind highlighting, soul consuming splendour easingly woke him. Centred ecstasy, groin impact, brain delivering. Quickly he became aware of Xaviera gently plumbing his sharply responsive mid depths for a viscous mouthwash interlude and acquiesced. He lay calm awaiting both payoffs.

"You should definitely stop drinking you know," she spoke eventually, her muffled tones to clarity reigned as her voice rose above the duvet, her head laying beside his now in the dank aftermath.

"What do you mean?"

"You should drink less," shaking her hair she reiterated.

"Why?"

"Why do you think? Because even your sperm tastes of alcohol!"

Someone smiled.

"But I like the altered state. I think better there. It's a nicer world," Fulke quietly implored.

"Surely you're not afraid of anything?"

"It's not that simple, doll."

"No, it wouldn't be, would it? Not if it's you."

"That's about it," he agreed.

Nostrils, now awake after exercise, met a take-away to throwaway staleness hung too long in the air. Even with the reduced capabilities of a smoker's nose Xaviera could bide it no longer and rose from the bed to clear away the non eaten morsels and switch on the powerful kitchen fan.

Fulke carried on sleeping although one eye noticed her movements. Watching her shapely calves and trim ankles shining in the sunlight as she changed support from one leg to the other in her heeled mules he wondered, what does she put on her skin?

Contemplation changed all that. Arms splaying out onto the bed-sheets he began inside. Our affair has been typical of a meeting that began hot and cooled to revive and cool again. It's like a sequel, a soap played out for ever, it's as if there is some kind of fated formula. Locked in bloody time. His mind now ambling along a great wall needing repair.

Of course it's a formula. Our conversation is formulaic, all love is formulaic, death is, a poem is. Her poems definitely are. Any tome is.

Thoughts amphetamined now.

Of course it's knowing the formula before one begins that is the secret. He snugly credited himself that he knew a few. Now just the one more with a strong structure is all he needs.

Xaviera expertly rolled a long joint and lit it. Luxuriously dragging on the spliff, pulling shiny pert lips in with her as she did so, to form a momentary thick, surreal cloud of smoke around her head and shoulders. The dusky, sweet smell caused Fulke to stretch over the covers again to enjoy the unusual sight watching her head with some curiosity to follow slowly down to her very short, lilac, cotton bathrobe-covered body as she began to prepare both a drink.

His smile disappeared, lost on the slow realisation that she claimed the genius of mankind is to be found in the pursuit of profit and comprehended his own sadness.

CHAPTER TWENTY FOUR

Rufus Rust was enjoying himself.

Here he was, sitting in the co pilot's couch in a light aeroplane flying along and above the South Coast, with confused thoughts of learning to sit in the other seat. Looking down from 2000ft, in only slight, variable winds with clear visibility for miles, onto the live map of the towns and cities and sea they pass, he wondered that up here the land seems lacking and insufficient, impersonal and endowed with inadequacy and no beauty down there can match the thrill of his new element.

R. Rust was on his way to an important morris dancing gig in the centre of Shoreham, as a business associate, Ralph Bore, knowing this and wishing to impress everyone in the known world, offered to fly him and a couple of his troupe to the spot, having first checked the long term weather forecast and solemnly informed the group that if they carried mobile phones they were definitely to be switched off on entering any plane, a CAA ruling not his.

This accomplishment had only been marred so far by the take off.

Of course Jimmy Pull, a clumsy, irritating member of the dance group, had to go to the toilet.

Again.

Just as the pre rotate checks were being undertaken he sheepishly enquired, adding he would not be long, although he called it a cloakroom like a Home Counties boy would, and of course he was sitting in the rear of the craft meaning others had to move before he could. His condition necessitated the plane taxiing back to the apron, switching off and placing chocks under the wheels to patiently wait for the weak bladdered.

J. Pull, fully relieved, entered the vessel the second time to everyone's irritation not shown or sensed. The vain aviator switched on again to move away with no result embarrassingly reflecting why there was no motion.

"Don't you think you better move those chocks before you go?" grinned the spotty faced, fringed apprentice coming out of the office to inform R. Bore of his mistake.

Behind the youth he could see grinning, uniformed faces at the windows. He tried to ignore them but found it difficult.

"Get out your side and pick up the chocks, will you, Rust? You can get out easier than me. I'll pull back the power while you do so, OK?" Ralph Bore said, too shamed to move.

"Yes, all right," Rust nervously spoke, too shamed to refuse.

"Just keep your head down that's all."

"Huh, yes, OK."

Rufus Rust was not totally sure this arrangement was fair or accurate, but very carefully wriggling along the ground like a lassoed snake did as he was told.

Take off experienced no other problems after that which was...

So in this white and green paint peeling Cessna 172, R. Rust was gazing out and down over Brighton wondering what the figure on top of that block of flats along Kingsway was doing with those birds nests. He presumed it was the caretaker doing one of his regular checks of the building. Or is it a St. Francis fanatical religious figure? He looks as if he's communicating very well with the seagulls. There's enough of them down there he assessed.

He was about to mention his discovery to Ralph when Danny Riddle tapped him on the shoulder and pointed out beyond the city towards the panoramic, green interland nearing an opera house and shouted, "That's where to dance, Rufus! On Glynde Hill!"

The four wore headphones capable of speaking to all.

"Where? Where's that then?" R. Rust relayed.

"Over there. Do you see? It's at four o'clock as they say up here. That's right, isn't it, Ralph?"

"It sure is," Ralph Bore answered, trying to sound mid-Atlantic, but was grateful to be asked something, anything. He wanted to belong.

Rufus Rust's thoughts hologrammed a vision of animated, Bacchanalian ecstasy as the dream tripped inside of the dance of a gig of the century on Glynde Hill.

"I can see it inside me, man," R. Rust said to D. Riddle.

"Me, too," Riddle replied.

"Yeah!"

"What's he doing on that roof?" R. Rust eventually talks to Ralph.

"I don't know." Ralph leans over insufficiently to view. "Lets go down and take a look, shall we?"

He pulls the power back to trim the plane into a steep, descending glide.

Why did I say that? R. Rust wondered as his stomach refuses to climb down with the plane and his ears feel pressurised to pop. He closes his eyes at the enormity of the sea rushing up to meet them, stopping himself calling out. The talked about man terribly occupied on the block of flats is unaware of their nearness and interest and does not see them as the Cessna 172 has straightened off at 150ft above sea level slightly below the roof of the building.

"Oh well! Not bad for a first try," monologued Ralph Bore.

"What does he mean, first try?" panicked R. Rust.

The high winged craft laboriously commenced ascending back to 2000ft, R. Rust finding the climb angle nervously uncomfortable. To his surprise he felt curiously safer after straightening out at the required height. He was not to think so long, though, as an interruption from the disturber among them commenced his extraordinary talent.

"Did you know I broke somebody's arm without knowing I'd done it?" said Jimmy Pull, the thin, long armed, broad shouldered farmer from the other back seat.

"Yes we did!" Rufus Rust exclaimed, watching the Albion view speed past much safer at this level. Still amazed he is in the air.

"There was an arm wrestling competition in my local, though I didn't know about it until I walked in the place."

"Here we go again," R. Rust speaks to the pilot.

The pilot did not reply, not wishing to get involved this time.

"So they all had a go and it seems one was absent from one team and they asked me if I would help out, so I did and I easily won this big bloke, who was the champion. Anyway, next night I goes down there for a drink and I'm told I broke Big Boy's arm, and he is a big piece of work. I can tell you. I didn't believe it until I saw him. The size of his biceps. Wow! Just as well it was a friendly match. Know what I mean?"

"We know what you mean," R. Rust placates.

The 172 takes a medium to steep, yoke pulled back, right turn, as Rufus Rust's facial expression enquires of Ralph Bore's concentrated forehead.

"There was a plane coming quite close, so I took action," Ralph Bore's relaxing features answer.

"There it is. Do you see it?" He points to a similar shaped craft several sky-miles from them quickly moving seaward to the left.

"Huh...Oh yes," replies shaken Rufus Rust.

Ralph Bore switches off the headphone connections to the two passengers behind.

Silence is heard between the remaining two. Ralph knows Rufus is going nowhere.

"Did I ever tell you how I learnt to fly, Rust?" Ralph enquires.

"Er...no," Rufus answers, thinking we have only spoken professionally so how could I know.

"Well I started in the glue factory county, you know?"

"Where?"

"Horse stealing country."

"I..."

"Essex."

"I...I didn't know."

"Yes. There. There's a byway, a path straight across the middle of the runway where people walk their dogs across and things like that, and you have to take off knowing this can happen. You're picking up speed while some old bloke is walking his mutt right in front of you, and the instructor says it'll be all right, he'll be gone by the time we get there!"

"Sounds fun," Rufus replies, thinking it does not.

"Another time we took off and the instrument panel fell out." Points down and ahead. "This block here! Quite disconcerting, I can tell you, when you're learning to fly."

"I can imagine," Rufus, beginning to want him to shut up as doubts to his own safety slowly sprout in his mind.

"Another time I was doing circuits, you know, land and take off practice around the airfield, and when I looked at the instructor he was asleep. Now that really filled me with confidence. He eventually wakes up and says, oh I had a bad night last night!"

R. Rust nods as much as his headset will allow, but worries more.

"I wouldn't mind, but next time he told me to go off on my own, be careful and don't bloody kill myself. If I'd been like him I probably would."

The conclusion of feelings. R. Rust definitely does not like this mode of transport.

"And taking off over water as well, I didn't like that. You take off and look down and all you see is sea. I didn't like that. I don't particularly like it now and I'm used to flying."

R. Rust decides less affirmed, the sooner silence.

"Shoreham Tower, this is Golf Bravo Oscar Lima X-ray." Rufus Rust realised Ralph Bore was no longer speaking to him, instead continuing his strange, dialectic use of the English language with others out there somewhere.

Ralph Bore was merely radioing ahead to facilitate their safe landing. His co pilot's seat heard a muffled but fuzzed reply to his sensibilities.

"Oscar Lima X-ray is a Cessna 172 four miles east of the field at 2200ft. Request joining instructions."

This new language omitting from R. Bore's mouth impressed R. Rust.

Again someone answered. Again Rufus Rust could not catch the words.

"There's the field! See?"

"Yes, I see!" Rufus Rust saw with his eyes closed. Rufus Rust worried.

"Low flying aircraft have to be careful not to hit high flying hills around this airfield," Ralph Bore smirked at R. Rust.

"They have?" R. Rust answers blind.

"It happens sometimes. Not usually fatal, though."

R. Rust coughs to gulp.

"That's...that's nice!"

The plane makes several steep turns he finds frightening but...

When he hears the power pulled back and Ralph Bore say, "Finals to land."

He knows. Now is the time to worry.

"Sweet Jesus save me! Please let it be all right! Let everything be all right!" Deep inside he feverishly repeats the phrases over and over. Simultaneously he endeavours to displace his fear, remembering he had never been the same since his cerealologist father died, mysteriously impaling himself on his favourite, psychedelic crop circle concocter 'The Magic Plane of Gawain' in the process of producing a series of complex geometrical Red Indian DNA structures during a warm May night in an earth energised oil seed rape field somewhere in the English deep south.

Ralph Bore the responsible aviator executes a textbook landing.

As the plane taxies from the runway to park Rufus Rust opens his eyes.

"Enjoy that?" asks Ralph Bore.

"You bet!" says Rufus Rust, already knowing he was catching a train back home.

All memory of the roof walking caretaker had forever vanished.

CHAPTER TWENTY FIVE

Fulke had become a frequent visitor to the abode of Xaviera and had familiarised himself with the well pitched, damp-proof, flat roof with its bold, clear guttering to off-load excess rain and the sad, decaying, mephitis inherent of the beast.

Only his second visit found him ascending the last, tasking treads to the metal roof door and successfully negotiating the plain, pointless, rusted bolt seemingly to feed the seagulls, loving the birds as he did. Though not a Chekov look-alike in sight, memories of his old soul mate were awakened as he slowly luxuriated in their summitted new company. Feathers soon reciprocated, understanding a soul brother instinctively.

Xaviera, knowing his detached wiles, took little notice of these heightened ruminations, instead staying below to dramatically compose 'The Birdman of Brighthelmstone'.

Above he hardly noticed the panoramic view of the northern French coast and half of England experienced from the height as he stared inward and elsewhere. Though reminding himself at regular intervals not to look over his shoulder as no-one was watching, no-one could see, and even the low flying aircraft along the sea-front flew lower than he presently walked. One time he supposed the noise of a plane near and low but never looked up to confirm presence.

There were old nests and new nests with some in busy use, but he wandered hoping and searching for the form with young eggs only, accessible and portable a small, untroubled distance. The flues to the, yes it was gas, central heating systems flowed out up here and once he had clarified which was hers, it was a simple case of placing a fertile nest over that flue. Warm being the weather the heating will not be set hence, any damage that carbon monoxide could cause would happen at a later date when he had left the area.

He knew a good murder when he saw it and had seen a few brilliant ones in his time. This would rate quite high in his perfection ratings, but overconfidence was looming like a gangrenous limp.

Gems appeared.

Like the Empire-believer of an aged janitor who, conveniently, had painful, rheumatic legs that never ventured on the roof, insisting it was someone else's job, preferring to rant at whoever is passing on how the country is going to the dogs.

Another sparkler.

No permanent residents of the other three penthouse homes to notice his skyward visitations.

So far so good.

He had observed many a perfect murderer be caught in the childish belief of superiority that no-one could catch them, hence he understood to keep the mind hungry and running.

The weather had to behave; no wild winds now becoming mini vortices whipping eyries away.

Life was becoming too perfect.

On every visit, be it daylight and clement weather, he had, assiduously and cautiously, sought the building's peak after the necessary, penthouse preliminaries. Attaching no significance to the predilectable quirks of any wind he would gaze solely into the East Sussex skies for long periods, until a frame of mind settled declaring hypnotically that these birds had been flying since time began. Behind wondering eyes, precociously aware of the development of the flying creature and its present ageless, buoyant beauty, his mind watched and catalogued how the gull swooped, glided to skim waves and verandas and noticed the movement from vertical flight to braking and hovering for seconds, only to enter a glide marvelling at the perfect landing system still a million technological miles away from man.

The birds perched so confidently close to him while he clearly distinguished darkened, tapered wingtips shading inwards to plump off white bodies, their feathers tapered aerodynamically relevant to direction and heard their excited human to deitic ponderous, facial expressions inevitably squawking out commands to all.

As if flying above all and everything in their feathery kingdom claimed them as the master race, a silent seagull conspiracy, a Rosicrucian rotary of elevated downdraughts.

His bewitched head hooked onto an aggregation of common gulls with an elitist air, herring gulls brake diving and smaller black headed gulls confusedly changing winter faces teeming and filling the heavens with proud, exaggerated flight in their airy temple of aesthetic, feathered fanaticism.

The conveniently nest sized, redundant vapour flue on which he had eventually placed the discovered fertile, seagull domicile was now truly obstructed to a substantial but partial seal, helped on by the extra bucket of mud he had struggled skyward with to ensure guaranteed fixture. He had, momentarily, considered using cement but luckily held all enthusiasm in check.

Hope was as high as the flying fowl feeling the warm air around the laying platform.

Success was in his future.

Necessary, because this was to be the last time he would meet her.

The decision had been taken.

They had copulated on this second coming together in a single lifetime on their first contact. Though be it the end of that first contact.

Differences astounded each in move, in smell, in touch, but there was to be no tabula rasa on either side, both having a mercenary end in view.

Fulke was perplexed and surprised as to why the love making was pleasantly contrasting, much time passing before the sole realisation that they were older and wiser, and an adrenaline rush whenever he thought of both futures, particularly her shortened one.

Their early meeting was as young and beautiful bodies knowing little difference and taking the world and themselves for granted. Now they take account of age and differences accumulated over the years, not always knowing why they do so.

And erudite delight was sweetening off.

As when urgently needing latrining, during a communal, complimentary session, he would initially rise from the consumatory rolls of evergreen white pillows and bedspread in the percolated pink and peachy coloured, sleeping room to catch his hair or body-part on her 'dream-catching shape changer' merely to smile at its superstitious values. " The knot goes on forever," she would sexily slur, horizontal under the goose feathered duvet on hearing the trembling token.

"I'm not in the mood to debate the point at the moment," he would invariably shout, with his body prescribing immediate action.

"The bad dreams are swallowed up and the good ones are reflected back to me," she continued.

He was in the bathroom by now splashing and listening too far away to comment.

Currently if she sermonised him on the predictable altercation he would no longer answer. As at present, he felt desire building up inside to wreck this sprawling, dangling fishing net in which were sown animal bones, glass balls, seashells, fishbones, animal horns and talisman shaped pieces of metal spread over a cornerwall of the bedroom, deeming it another sad, pathetic, hippie obstacle he was forced to contend and conquer.

Each looked down, sexually appreciating the shape of the other's body under the thin thread, summer clothing, sunk into the car seats, feeling the heat of the engine accompanied with the random smell of fuel. Fulke found it worrying still being in the same amorous mood after the long afternoon spent together, though he was in no doubt that he would still go through with the foolproof plan. She found herself believing she was in love with him again, but dismissed the whimsical introspection after a few moments.

Instead, she stretched over to help herself to one of his dashboarded lozenges simply enjoying the drill that emphasised her tight dress knowing he would notice.

A meal Shoreham way was all he said as they stepped into Treblinka.

Low dark cloud, rain heavy but when to release, hung over like a lid with the edges leaking late, chrome yellow sunlight. Through the passenger glass Xaviera poetically equated huge rocks near the shoreline as lozenges, soothing and settling the sea-waters, but felt nothing for the modern, minimal mimicry of the dock architecture they passed. Near and distant coastal lights emitted their private, luminous chills. The couple drove by an uncrowded, cheerless, MacDonalds fast food restaurant surprisingly without anti capitalist comment flowing from passionate mouths, and noticing a pavement drunk only lurching in the way of well dressed types daring himself to rip or not to rip off.

Fulke took out a long, cigar shaped, metal cylinder with *'Roche Drugs'* displayed on the side. He produced a large, effervescent pill and enclosing it in his mouth began to suck the tablet, like a child with a sweet, experiencing a natural high as the juices sprung up into his nasal cavities.

"What are you doing?" Xaviera enquired, seeing his face muscles play.

"I'm taking vitamin C."

"Do you imagine you're unhealthy then?"

"Not particularly. I just don't want my leakages or droppings to taste of alcohol that's all."

Xaviera smiled. Her shoulder moved slightly closer to his.

An equable evening of good food, with both pleasantly satisfied by the many creative choices to suit their different tastes. Unparalleled conversation, their own and non-stop smiling Italian piano accordion entertainment occurred in a greenbelt pub, lost in the landscape interior behind the port that had long since gone to the dogs on the money trail as Fulke understood it, and instead concentrated on excellent meals at the expense of beer.

Xaviera smiled as Fulke quietly ranted in his unmistakable, unrestrained manner at most things wretched humanity spoil. Any anthropologist studying them with their usual concentration of patronising arrogance would have guessed a long married, happy couple on an anniversary date.

After the meal.

Variety.

Another narrow, winding drive further up country to where Fulke joyfully deemed a bucolically buried, rustic pub, meaning minus a jukebox, fruit machines and video games and plus old men playing dominoes with ageing dogs under their seats, old women supping stout in half pint glasses and frightening amounts of alcohol once again the culture of youth. Where on sitting Fulke noticed the dramatic, blood-red ceiling of the bar area contrasting with the peeling, white painted walls and untreated, dry-rot jump.

Because of the limited, cream bulb lighting, the vibrant overhead seemed like a sensational set from some cannibalistic beyond horror film, as it drenched the room red, seemingly expecting body parts to push through the glistening, gloss paint. Everyday objects reflected on this upper side seemed to transform into 'Poltergeist' extras.

"Maybe the landlord is a defrocked surgeon, caught sewing body bits together, now hiding deep in the Sussex Downs from the condemnation of the Medical Council," Fulke laughed to Xaviera.

"Shut up will you, Fulke, please! Talk like that gives me the creeps, especially when I'm gazing up on a roof like this. Especially in the depths of the country, and it's dark outside, with no street lights!" she implored.

He grinned.

The beer did not want to slide down as easily as normal. He knew he should not have eaten all that delicious steak, any of that delicious steak. Meals ruin a good drink, any drink. He thought he had absorbed that crock of wisdom years ago.

Two drinks in they leave.

Because he feels bloated.

Xaviera does not mind, being able to take or leave the public house atmosphere.

Back in the car pre ignition, they meet close.

Both of his hands adapted themselves to her bodyline as they descended her still-impressive form. She traced a similar tender compliment pectorially apexing.

For a half minute they held each other tight.

"My period's late. Really late," she whispered the disclosure.

His hands hung unceremoniously in the air. Sheered, stupefied and stunted.

His mind said, but….

His mouth answered nothing.

The aphrodisiac highs in the dramatic situation spilled to the lowest, to a fatigued substructure.

Behind them the rain began to stream down the rear window to eventually shroud the full vehicle, causing Fulke to re-run the windscreen wipers before driving away Brighton bound.

Miming subdued emotion they concluded their last automobile ride together.

CHAPTER TWENTY SIX

He left late and drunk.

He left her late and drunk.

Xaviera was in bed sleeping when he sneaked out of her flat, quietly closing the plum quilted door and making sure it locked on the inside as he heard the comforting chank cluck of greased, mechanical exactness. He hit the wall only twice walking down the short, dimly lit, concrete coloured corridor to the lift button. On the second knock he remembered that the insincere one of a couple makes the tenderest speeches on parting, and knowing he had done so must fulfil a Proustian prophecy of sorts.

Pressing the knob and listening to the hoist rushing to meet him Fulke pondered on all the oil in the world, then why hasn't someone used more of it on this machine?

The mechanism tiredly clicked into position, too loudly it seemed to him, feeling guilty already when he briskly entered its shiny, cubed space. Depressing the ground level L.E.D. glowing counters he relaxed, accepting that all good things must come to an end. Only to be interrupted when five floors from his destination the descending apparatus stopped.

Fulke hit a few buttons but nothing worked.

Panic enveloped him like premature burial as he imagined someone noticing what was going on. Schweibb Sweitt sweat poured down his energised brow.

Suddenly he stopped.

A breakthrough of realisation occurred in that there is no rush of any kind for anything. So slow down all and everything. If anything does happen it is weeks away in the cold months of the year when the heating is used, and the only reason he is not going to see her up to that time is so he will not be suspected of the tragic accident that will occur.

She is, after all, like the rest of us. She came from a random birth and will suffer a random death. He felt better on thinking that.

The badly maintained lift clanked some more and recommenced the descent. Fulke smilingly shrugged his wide shoulders.

Walking down the steps of the long building, the scent of catpiss and nettles travelled on the light wind to purge his approaching senses. Bitter to bitterer. Unprocessed, exposed nature in the raw. Paying back time when nature exhales instead of man's machines. Showing the human race how to do things correctly.

Refreshing the world.

Their world.

As he slouched towards 'Treblinka,' kicking up the damp, uneven gravel, a clear glint of moonlight on disturbed metal informed him that a wing mirror had been disturbed to beyond tensile strength and was hanging too awkwardly down the side of the car.

"What impoverished, intellectually stunted, emotionally crippled, feeble minded, coprophagous wanker did this, I wonder?" mumbling to no-one.

Having safely gaffer taped up the wing mirror, not wanting to be stopped for something so insignificant, he began the drive back to Hastings knowing it was near the time the squad car shifts change on most of the route. He knew people and their habits. It was his job.

Acceptance slowly emerged inside, knowing he had enjoyed this evening and their other times together even so and despite. He told himself for the fiftieth time that night that he was useful to society, socio-artistically useful now to complement his day job, and he believed the literary world had been done a favour.

He was sure of it.

Switching on the window screen wipers before negotiating the complex junction near the Palace Pier to counteract spots to streams of rain refracting sight, and telling himself to watch Treblinkas mannerisms in this changed weather, he turned onto Marine Parade. Wet roads and the car's light, back wheels had never held a truce, hence corners cautiously gauged, far away from slipping and sliding ratios.

Fingers hit the tape.

Bat Chain Puller explored the night.

The act unusual, in that he normally pressed the tape button before switching the ignition, yet tonight he had driven a couple of miles before the thought of entertainment jostled to the lead.

He slowly realised he was becoming impossibly restless, and wondered if the accident, the deed would be tonight what with the weather changing to wet, hence damp, thus cool. After all, it could be any night soon.

The sea front route took Treblinka speedily passed Roedean School for Girls and prudently low geared down the hill to Rottingdean village. But not before a noisy skid across the road upon the commencement of the decline to conclude dangerously close to the cliff edge suggested the revised approach.

Fulke decided to stop.

To reassess dramas of the mind.

He halted on the seaside car park at the bottom of the steep incline.

Love Lies was playing quietly as he left the car to study the placated sea and the beginning of another wondrous dawn. The calmness of the moment caused his mind and body to cautiously tilt back on Treblinkas bonnet, enjoying the warmth of the engine against the damp morning.

He kept tilting.

Way back into his world history.

To become acutely aware of how family gave him strength.

Half closed, tired eyes analogised with the mind. The projector at the back of his skull dawdled into action. His childhood and before began to roll like an old, familiar, comforting film.

Fulke stood, reclining, watching as his family soap topped his ratings...

Recollections of his mother talking filled his unsteady, swimming thoughts. He heard her again telling him how they both travelled though he only part travelled being born on the moving train across the ransacked, continental land mass until they reached still free England, seeing those White Cliffs of Freedom permanently watching darkest Europe.

She spoke again of his grandfather, his father's father, how he had escaped from prison hospital in Russia helped by a woman friend, but never why he was imprisoned in the first place.

Fulke was not sure his beloved parent knew the whole story. Some terrible even horrific violence was hinted at and mused on in their long intimate chats, sat huddled for warmth in their two-roomed Dover council flat extolling an exclusive view of an exterior, minimalist brick wall, but she communicated no clarity of narrative and he never enquired, respecting her stifled wishes or ignorance of the event.

Thoughts stumbled on.

To the recounted tale of his starving grandparent along with other desperate drifting folk stealing a golden Jesse tree from a Welsh Russian millionaire and selling it to White Russian antique dealers for an urgent profit. Eventually Tsar Death permanently staked his forefather who left a surviving son, his father, to eventually escape from the lunacy and savagery, derangement and discord to the moderately safer Poland after the left wingers of the world rejoiced at the Soviet Proletarian Revolution.

On crossing the border Pater changed his name from Kranikoslov to many other names to finally settle on Sweittervil at his future wife's suggestion though Fulke never understood any of their reasons. Father Leon learnt to fly in the Free Poland Airforce knowing borders of countries were suddenly important again, until one day noticing his one love, the permanent Papirosa cigarette smokiing Zlata Zachariah the Lithuanian street-fighter wandering in her delicious, idealistic hope through their permanently, on alert airbase carrying a guaranteed plan of escape that changed.

All the time.

His parents knew each other throughout a chaotic time.

They had initially met in a street battle between communists and fascists.

Love at first fistfight.

Had married late in life in eventual peacetime but in Germany and nevertheless begot.

Begun to begot.

But only the one.

Mother told him some of their romance.

How his peripatetic poppa had called her his 'Zany Zlata', zigzagging through her idiosyncratic Zionism cleverly in and out of ideologies open and closed and occasionally interwoven. His beloved Zlata had appeared to work for the German High Command and donned their smart black SS Panzerjacke uniform *female officer version* with compulsory shiny black leather marching boots *marschtiefel.*

A sight his patriarch allowed himself to be seduced by in his dark, weak, excited moments.

Even after the war.

In this disguise mother laboured relentlessly for the/any underground and the Allied Alliance being greatly honoured after the war to that effect.

Having joined the British Royal Air Force as a Polish Pilot in the War to survive with honours, his father fatally crashed on 15 August 1949 when one of the engines of his Douglas D.C.3 Dakota decided to quit on finals while flying the Berlin Airlift just one day before the operation ceased.

And without ever knowing his offspring.

The pregnant Sad Madonna needed to go on.

Zlata devised another plan as she travelled.

All the flyers wore Irving flying suits, helmets and oxygen masks, meaning thick sheepskin jackets and trousers to keep out the cold, yet all arrived back with mutterings of heat swiftly removing the hot garments hence sweat or schweibb or the between where she hung her syntax strategy. She kept hearing similarities in the words, or thought she did when pilots of all nationalities and languages landed on their mercy missions.

"Jesus, Irvil! I sweat!"

A common refrain, but one she could use to protect her offspring from the world.

She heard the German, American English and British English sound similar here so supposedly no-one would notice. Some noise in between she would use to sound upper-class English as she viewed it, the country already decided on.

Meaning the prize.

American pilots with fancy, safe, cautious sounding monocles like Irvil and Virgil and Arvin and Irvin drawled monotonously of the heat while the British quietly cursed remaining exclusive.

Minds move.

As Zlata's did when she produced what she insisted was a guarantee of success in the British class system. Place the two altered words together and hyphenate them. *Sweitt-ervil.*

Eureka, the hope goes on.

She wanted the best for her babe and this was the answer. Two innocent words hooked close for life to become power. To lose forever the Soviet Kranikoslov. Hope sprung for mater and spirals for all.

Zlata had always studied English literature with a passion born out of deficit and named her child accordingly. He never got used to her false teeth, though. Never bringing himself to look her fully in the face for any length of time. They made her mouth big so it seemed to him while the old browning photographs of her, he remembered, showed a prettier, more compact, confident smile. But there was a silly fashion in those days in those cultures for a woman to have all her teeth out and false ones inserted as speedily as the mouth allowed in the belief that teething problems would be a thing of the past.

An economic and pain-ridding prize all realised.

Fulke liked to think he followed this family tradition of strength, patience and tenacity that would help him through his current, strained period. There was something to be said for the partial, parental eugenics practised in the old countries after all.

In atavism we trust.

Grid patterned Peacehaven collectively slept its dream of fearful normalisation until Treblinkas lights actioned the beginning of more fanciful invents in the collective sleeping consciousness. Nightmares of double-barrelled Post Office robberies came to fearful minds.

Fulke fast forwarded **Hair Pie: Bake 1,** sometimes checking the road ahead as he did so.

After all there were corners to incurve ahead.

He needed lyrics.

Lonely was an instrumental this time in a morning.

Moonlight on Vermont began to quickly soothe.

Newhaven cleared trouble free. Climbing out the ferry port's valley, following the right turn to Seaford, he glanced to the left and saw, positioned slightly back, a sleeping camp of roadside vagrants, their part time jobs entail hustling lay-byed car personnel for survival items with the occasional lucky bonus of seduction on a foolishly parked supermarket container driver.

During the drive and particularly now on reaching Bulverhythe, the edge of town but a mile or so from the centre, he had decided that he would head for Bo's flat to seek out purgatory in her pudendum as family genetics he knew would not let him sleep.

Parking Treblinka on Devonshire Road, he undid her sidedoor with his key and treaded in gently no longer noticing the damp morning air. Cursing, he realised the hippies were in this weekend with their ashram antics, so he stayed downstairs awake while his woman meditated and relaxed and person centred the gullible guests. She takes them from their journey without to their journey within finding themselves on their tantric way above, below and inside out, or so she described to him, and always looking down on themselves as they so do.

He argued back stoically that it was clearly hippie shit. But they were upstairs now, chanting some shaman's mantra and all he wanted to do was sleep, as his slowing metabolism was frantically indicating.

CHAPTER TWENTY SEVEN

Fulke noticed the kitchen washing machine full of programmed, purified and purged garments ready for alfresco aeration and felt male panic.

To hang out or to ignore.

Positively he found the calico peg-bag and began to carry clothes from the appliance out to her backyard for airing on the line. He knew not to peg necks of shirts or clumps of cloth together when wet, but spread out the folds to openness so as to freshen speedier and thorough. Bo's cats, Gorky and Rothko, were soon around his ankles causing unsteady footwork. The two tortoise shelled felines remonstrating rampant hunger with the remedy nowhere to be found.

"All right. I'll see what there is," he affectionately informed them, walking inside.

They followed him, gazing upwards, as he mother hubbarded their food cupboard.

"All right. All right. I'll fetch you some. Hold on," his voice fighting through the frantic purring.

Outside heading for an open all hours shop close to St. Andrews Market, he turned onto South Terrace to see closing ahead a tall, emaciated and pale young man, arms hanging by his sides with an extended paunch not unlike an umbrella way over his black combat trousers appear out of the Terrestrial Tabernacle of Cosmic Creators open doorway and walk towards him.

"What about me? What about me? What about me? What about me? What about me? What about me?" His voice stretched and strained in a monotoned, aqueous anguish, like an emotionally, neglected robot looking for the breaking point.

"Change the tape pal, will you?" the overtired Fulke replied, not in the mood, thinking this was another Old Town Week act and noticing as he did so the tattooed letters above the knuckles on both the lad's bony fingered hands,

J E S U and **L O V E**,

And how the two middle fingers permanently curled inwards advertising future discomfort.

"What about me? What about me?" Mountebank mania moved on.

"What about you? Who the hell are you?" Fulke provoked now.

"You bastards. You've been questioning my old man again, haven't you? You lot! My mother! You're all after him! Say he's done things he hasn't!" the lad cried the words. "If he had, wouldn't I know? Wouldn't I? Too right I bloody would. He never did anything to me. Never. You all stitched him up, but why? Why? Why?"

The malodour of stale, recently digested, cheese and onion crisps influenced Fulke's nostrils. Similar scents never bothered him when he smoked regularly, hence at times like this he seriously considered starting again.

Behind the lamenting figure D.I. Swettervil noticed several large banners aside an offset Union Flag leaning or held with limited permanence to the stone wall. 'The Celestial Times' newspapers were on sale alongside large apocalyptic posters displayed on the ochre-coloured temple front advertising *The Legacy of Jesus - Healing All Illnesses by Faith - JOHN WAYNE BITTER will cure YOU*

"Look, if you have a complaint see the station sergeant. I'm off duty." D.I. Swettervil endeavoured to walk on irritated. There was an unknown sordidness he could not fathom about the insistent young man making Fulke's whole being uncomfortable, and this was definitely not the place or the time to conduct enquiries with such a volatile interviewee.

Completely aware of his own vulnerability, he felt one of his socks slip down and his failing fastidiousness finally leave him. The heightened tension even told him there was no dandruff on his black jacket collar despite its fondness for a sprinkle. For the first time in his life he would prefer to pursue a case with others. Whatever this case turned out to be, if it was to be a case.

"That's it. All excuses. Please leave him alone. You know he's not involved in this case. You know who is and it's not my old man. So why bother upsetting him? Just because he's a bit simple," the youngster persisted.

Two large, crucifix-tattooed, baseball-capped, well anodised men had stepped out of the church as if to care for rather than rescue the young man. One carried a blue and white bomber jacket, that the detective's mind remembered from somewhere, to cover the young man's white shirted chest. Fulke noticed impressive biceps bulging under their 'White Jesus' T shirts lacking underarm deodorant, damp-down spray necessitated since their recent enthusiasm in a less than spiritual tussle terrorising white magic elders and warlocks in a tavern somewhere close.

Approaching each side of their leader one sentinel reverentially spoke, "Don't go upsetting yourself, master. You have a service to do later today and you need all your energy for healing your flock."

"Yes. Please come along in, John." The other guard.

"He's a famous faith healer, you know," to Fulke. "Why do you go and upset him? He heals the terminally sick, all the cripples and the insane," the first pleaded.

"Me?!!!!!" Fulke spluttered. Having no time or energy for argument, not even to laugh at the claim as he still had not slept, he turned and tried to keep on walking.

"He laid on the Turin Shroud, you know, and it fitted him," Lash, the second attendant, said.

"What?! But it's behind thick glass on a wall. How the hell could he?" Fulke turned and found himself replying to the facile comments.

"There are ways. There are always ways," said Shilling, the first minder.

Introspective thin clothed, thin soled 'doleys' trio past on the other side of the street like a chain gang hunched in homage to paucity. In the same landscape, but another reality. Neither group see the other.

The lad stopped bleating now as if realising the hopelessness of pleading with a policeman for appropriate behaviour within the law, and produced from a back pocket a pamphlet which he handed to the other side.

"We have family who will help dad's fees, and I don't mean the church. I will make myself visible by writing my religious tracts and I will be recognised." The lad spoke entranced behind his rictus of hysteria.

As he did so his slightly curved spine permitted his hands to rest on his paunch as if this fast food development was a separate piece of furniture built for that exclusive purpose.

Then quieter, "My parents never cared, touched or loved."

Fulke, not understanding or desiring to do so, took the leaflet speedily in the hope that the gesture would afford him needy relief. It seemed to work, and the lad with companions began to walk slowly back to the place of worship renovating his war-cry as he moved.

"What about me? What about me? What about me? What about me?" The teutonic moog moved sound around again.

"Master. Please reserve your strength for your next healing session," one minder spoke.

The hermeneutic helpers finally helped their messianic healer into the temple.

Slowly the noise faded as Fulke finally, definitively, turned the next corner thinking something happened elsewhere, and all the weirdoes and nutters really do come to the coast for their care in the community as they surely do not all originate here.

Realising he was carrying the handout he looked down at the sweat stained, donated comicstrip of superstitious scribbling, a plagiarising pamphlet printed by The Society against World Jewish Domination and Hebrew Conspiracies, and noticed badly drawn cartoons of truckers, strongmen and motorbikers all wearing Jesus tattoos, and how tough guys can love Jesus tattoo.

The next waste bin existentially accepted the brochure's descending circular flight.

Despite being a street away D.I. Swettervil could still faintly hear the young man's manic haunting strains as he started to sing in a noteless voice, "Oh did those feet in ancient times walk upon England's mountains green?" as a part sob, part obsession, part life therapy, and at the same time drinking in power, but from where?

Fulke did not like admitting, especially to himself, that this act made him uneasy and shivered, feeling neck hair rise responding to the aching noise, slowly realising his stomach communicated a pained emptiness.

He knew he had lost, but why? What was it that worried him?

Walking, he began remembering where he had seen the lad before. He had been up for fighting drunk a few times, and there was one they could not prove about him and a female cousin of his. That included his father too in some implied way and he was jailed for it. Fulke remembered a large bail had been vainly put forward by the name Hume.

He wondered the obvious.

Turning the corner and entering the Ever Open shop selling all from dogfood, to headache cures, to tinned, sliced peaches in syrup with every variation in-between self evident Of course! He remembered the police had been talking to the lad's father, along with every other irresponsible man in town that had been punished, about the recent murder on the hill.

A bell rang as he entered the garishly coloured premises of commercial plenty.

A young man jeaned, straggle haired and T shirted was talking to the proprietor. "I'll have two of those at 99p."

"Sorry, sir?"

"I'll have two of those at 99p."

"But they're not 99p, sir."

"Oh, right, uh. Have you got any stamps?"

The customer replaces the two medium sized, dark chocolate bars.

"Yes, sir."

"Uh, first class or second class?"

"Yes. All prices sir."

"Uh, first class. Two first class."

"Right, sir. Two first class stamps. Anything else?"

His brown fingers tear off the number.

"Oh, I'll take this bar and the stamps."

The customer picks up one of the dark chocolate bars.

"And the gum, sir?"

"No, just this chocolate and the stamps."

"And the gum sir?"

"Hey?"

"The gum, sir, the gum. In your other hand."

The customer looks in that direction.

"Oh! I didn't know. Sorry. I wasn't trying to nick it or anything. Really."

"That's all right, sir."

"Sorry. Sorry. No, I didn't mean anything."

"That's all right, sir."

"I'm sorry. Really."

"That's OK, sir. That will be 92p."

The shopkeeper waits while the customer jean searches for the amount. The potentially guilty reaches deep in his pocket, retrieves money only to spill coins onto the floor. He bends down to re-collect first picking up all coins of value. A penny is lifted and suddenly aware of being scrutinised, he drops the base coinage back on the ground leaving two other pennies remaining there. Standing position regained he pays quietly and leaves.

The proprietor's tensed face slowly smiles on seeing Fulke.

"Mr. Swettervil, sir, and how are you?"

"I'm fine I guess, Mr. Bhatia, but that," pointing to the door, "it still goes on I see."

"It does. I get too much of that sort of thing and if you excuse me, Mr. Swettervil, sir, the police don't support me at all. No matter how much I complain."

"I know. I don't know how you stick it, I really don't. It's like a combat eighteen meeting place this is."

"Thank you for your honest assessment of the situation, Mr. Swettervil, sir. Can I get you anything?" The trader attempts officious tones but melts as quickly.

"Oh, two of those tins please." Fulke points to the stacked to please catfood containers.

The counterman fetches the weight.

"And a box of Fisherman's Friends, please."

"That'll be £1.52p thank you, Mr. Swettervil, sir."

"We know the one who's just left. He's been up before for housebreaking. I recognised him." Fulke feeling frighteningly inadequate.

"So do something about it, please, Mr. Swettervil!"

"We do what the law allows us to do and that's all."

They both smile stoicism at each other. A sudden bond of mature comprehension and fatalistic understanding joins the two on an equal understanding of the complexities of existence and the lack of reason therein.

"Goodbye, Mr Swettervil, sir."

"See you, Mr. Bhatia."

Back tracking to Bo's flat he risked surviving dog detritus to shoe soles and gazed up instead.

The sky looked good, pavements had dried, the sun shone like a smile and clouds stayed with rain. Behind him he thought he heard an echo-chambered voice saying, "May the angels forgive you," but looking behind he saw no-one there.

Passing a billboard he read:

WHAT A LIFE!
BIRTH
JESUS
DEATH
AFTERLIFE!

CHAPTER TWENTY EIGHT

Malcolm Lowry knew tonight being yet another Carnival Night might lead to the abbreviation of a boozed interland, but what to do?

Stick to your local haunts, he mused.

"A bottle of whisky, Malc?" the landlord said.

"No. Just...just...just a pint, Corporal, please. It's gonna be a long night this day of the dead. This day and night of the topers. This day of the night of the wiggerly wobberly walk!"

"Flash barmen in this country," Malcolm loudly mentioned to his companion, "it's getting more like the Colonies everyday! I wonder can their monochrome wit imbibe them with a gift for muteness and strict accordance with customers wishes?"

To the failure with liquids he darkly eloquenced. "The night is the daliant father of the morning. Do your mazed murmurs presume acceptance of darkened dreams of realities?...Read up on your post structuralist thought, pal, and hurry with my sustenance."

"Did you see that Beckett film last night?" the bar boy pruned confidently.

The fool wishes to patronise, but on Malc went.

"Beckett? What channel was that supreme valediction of truth screened?"

"Number four at ten."

"Don't be ridiculous! I was getting ratarsed discussing Schopenhaurian pessimism with this superbly stoical and studious Irishman from the Hebridean colony in a quiet little snug of a bar across the river, wouldn't you concur, Raymond?"

"I...I...I...er I, er believe that is correct," spoke his grinning, brown toothed, unshaven companion. "We had, er, what can only be described as, er, a hell of a night."

"We, as an intellectual duo, that is, celebrate the wanton beverage in this Babylon never seeking to denounce it," Malc goes on, "To drink it dry and move on is our sole inclination."

The Hebridian of Irish vintage continued. "Malcolm, er, here has a talent, which we, ah, both share, of, er, gently creatively fusing and exhuming before rejecting, er, surplus literary liquid enthusiastically though, ah, never in public."

Perplexed to revenge there was only one last cheap retort the bar bloke knew, and he flogged it to contextual death in one rhetorical. "You been talking to Matthew Lewis again then Malcolm?" As he commenced removing Malcolm's almost empty glass presuming it was dead.

Malc said and thought nothing for an instant.

Suddenly he grabbed the owner's hand with his pint glass still moving there, and spoke slowly with the tremble, force and surprise of a crop circle denouncer. "Don't you ever try and take the piss again avatar of slime! Or I promise I'll slap you bad... Always remember landlords are the lowest fucking scum on the planet!"

The room watched quietly.

The landlord did too.

Fortunately for prevailing moods the boozer was noisily invaded by a selfish, juvenile throng competing with each other to be served first.

Malcolm lurched even closer to the jump.

A new mood.

"Gotta find somewhere quieter before the night has won. Harridans spinning in the air are everywhere. Is this fuel for a future limited edition? An idol to contemplate, adulate and revile is a journey through heated forests and cooled oceans spinning into somebody else's gehenna.

Maybe I'll try 'The Wellie', trade's not too busy there, but tonight who knows. You accompanying genius, Raymond?"

"I..I..I'll be over later, Malcolm. I have business to attend to," replied his confederate.

"What you need to do, you do, but first contemplate," Malc replied, finishing his shant.

"Indeed. I will do just so, er, that's right!"

The carnival-goers watched, hypnotised in awe as Malcolm moved towards the door like a pinball scoring off everything he hit. With no tilt given and on his third attempt he walked through and not into the doorposts. Applause was heard, but not by the writer; he was either on the next street or another world asleep in the gutter dreaming of darkness and last judgements.

The landlord was not committed to celebration.

He knew Malc too well.

Fulke recognised the slope of the shoulder, the contour of the paunch, the misshapen, misappropriated talent as it hung limboed between the pavement and the road over from the Old Town churchyard. He helped his friend to a form of standing.

A far easier sentence to write than to physically enact.

They were drinking friends of old. Fulke knew there was always round two...or three...or...at any rate he'd be talking to Malc again very soon. This he could guarantee. The shants would rise again. In minutes. And by the time they had reached or fallen towards the next pub, The Wellington.

Drinks were purchased and seats staked deliberately away from the people who always have a story to tell.

"I was born too late, you know, Fulke. At the spiralled spinning end of the great adventure that was the exploration of the earth."

Fulke was not going to listen to much of this.

"You know that pub on Beachy Head burnt down, don't you Malc?"

"Yes, I think so. Do I?"

"Well, they've now built a restaurant in its stead, so that suicides can now have their Last Supper with their families before they jump. Or the whole family can decide to take the plunge together."

Malcolm chuckles.

Fulke knew Malcolm needed something so he provided.

"Sylvia out tonight?" he enquired of the master.

"I don't know. We will see her around no doubt."

"Not seeing Ted, is she?"

"Fucking hope not. What a fucking slapper he turned out to be. I can say that being the writer. I'm not leaping into brash sunlight but stretching other dark extremes."

"You and me both, brother."

"What do you mean, Fulke?"

"Something serious, Malc. You can both listen when you're both here. It's easy to assimilate."

"What have you done, Fulke?"

"Oh, it will out as we go. We're together on this night, we're drinking and minds go forward and back, but my gleam in the sunlight is a prize. My prize."

"You confuse still. Never mind. I lay a claim in my work to *the* prize. I lay and say that original work is only and merely so. We all know the obscurities. Would you knowing that someone else has used your work, even though I know someone has used your work and you've used other's work, but my only claim is that someone has used my work."

"Get the agents onto it, don't you, Malc. That's all I know."

"I'm usually too fucking pissed to care, Fulke."

"You're not listening, Malc."

> What a surprise
> difficulties arise
> at this altercation's
> abbreviation.

"Malc. We're serious now."

"What's happened? Happening?" Malcolm's mind had wandered outside but was back.

"You're listening?" Fulke drinks a third of his pint in one gulp.

"Naturally, and I'm not judging. One thing I never would." Re-lights the pipe of drugged obsequies.

"Thanks, Malc. Malc." Fulke moves from the enveloping smoke.

Holding the pipe like a voodoo doll Malc volumes. "So spill. Believe me, no rotter ever told me a banjoistic gleam to polish my devil's eye."

"How about I thought about the dead end of another? How about I contemplated a desire to do precisely so? How about I made graphically and physically sure that a person would not live?"

"So this is your heaviness. What a lark you are. You imagine I haven't been there? Who's buying by the way?"

Malcolm as accurate as usual, notes both pint glasses are unadorned mikva.

"I'll buy as I want to know your verdict."

"Cheers!" Malc chimed to the new beers and admitted that he sometimes shouted, "le chiem" as people thought he was a Jew, though he himself did not give a fuck.

The door opened differently.

No noise, mere motion.

Sylvia walked in.

Resplendent in teeth no-one could emulate, literary behaviour no-one could stretch their mind to and sexuality no woman could hope to reach. Our hero was moved to loin preparation as falling in love was an unbelief he clung to, but still on she walked as in a dream. His private vision. *"Born too late,"* Fulke sang sweetly in her direction, noticing her drinking in the moment. He had loved this as a juvenile and it was here still. A liberty to lead his person. Sedate, supreme and superior. Sylvia seemed the dream of all and everything in literary quarters. It was a dream they all habitually hung, drawn and lectured on their courses

197

allowing her damp grass to weep on their shoes. Why didn't she mention the type of shoes? Or were they boots?!

He composed himself before such pulchritude.

"Sylv, how's the prose? Ted still cleaning you out?" Malcolm, viewing the new presence through separate eyes, pushed a social enquiry, though not wondering the answer.

"We're drinking. Let's talk. You're the only two guys I love. With no cameras we could and would make love and everything too, too many times," she replied with the urbaneness of her talent.

"So the usual?" Fulke offers.

"Pint of Guinness, that's correct. Though there's a biological statement soon to say that females can take half the liquor, but on we go."

"We do love, don't we? But how?" Fulke murmured.

"Seen Xaviera recently, Fulke?" Sylvia polite as usual.

"Er..Why do you ask?"

"No reason. Only I met her recently."

"Oh, did you? I..I've seen her a couple of times, I guess, but only a couple."

"All right. I believe you, Fulke. I do."

"You used to there, didn't you, Fulke, old boy?" Malc rejoins the main event of the evening.

"Please, you both listen or maybe not?" Fulke begins emptying his heart.

Malc and Sylvia in confer are now open to admissions and apologies beyond their dreams.

"How are you both on morals?"

"Huh!!" In guttural unison.

"Do you say, as I say, that there is a fine line to be drawn? Even though I'm not sure where the line is drawn. Do you ever clarify any points or belief beyond stardom or rationality?"

"Are we both listening? We are!"

"Do either of you ever feel the need to remonstrate against another for copying your work? Or anyone else in that position for that matter?"

"You began something the other night, did you not, Fulke? Is this the same burden?"

"Yes, Malcolm, it is."

"You see, you've been through some similar false guilt, right?" Fulke looks towards Malcolm who shrugs acquiescently. "Though you know, Malc, any work you acquired or spilt quickly and uniquely became your own no matter what?" Malcolm shrugs again.

"Sylv, I know he always does get away with everything because of his genius and I know he will always do, but I'm taken to new drastic steps."

"How shall I say?" Sylvia replies. "I committed dramatic suicide and my two timing lover said I merely slipped on a banana skin in parapraxis. To see how far I'd go, you know?"

"We know."

"That's what can happen with the ultimate statement," she continued. "I'd give up, but it's too late for me. Tell us more Fulke. This is truly fascinating!"

"If you're sure you want to know."

"We're sure." The four shoulders look at each other.

"You know my status as a shy scribe?"

"We do."

"And how I keep my work close? Well, this belief has nourished me through the years knowing no-one will see my work. Except present company naturally. So imagine my belief when my work is seen commercially, by me, in a poetry book, acknowledged by another."

"I knew you could do it," Malc pleasures, misunderstandingly.

"Whoa, Malcolm!" Sylv cries.

"Too late for that now. I wasn't amused by it so guess what happens next?"

"It's another art against capitalism example, according to your gospel," Malcolm ears to Fulke.

"That's right, Malc, it is. So, Sylv. Is it OK for me to do it?"

"There's a person here who breathes, smiles and loves, Fulke."

"There's a person here that cheats, Sylv."

"Well, Fulke. I don't want to know the name. It is a sine qua non in your artistic development within this culture. So it's a maybe."

"Christ, you've changed, Sylv!"

"I did not change. My world did. Jesus! Even Ted developed a blood sports bent in his later days."

Malcolm cannot stay quiet here and laughs, but not before complementing Sylvia on her poetic phrasings.

"Whose turn is it?" Malc looks at both.

"Mine, I suppose," Fulke looks forlorn.

"No, it can't be! I'll do it! There's a band I gotta go see this carnival week, too." Syvia, not wanting to stay with the current theme, attempts movement, collecting up their glasses.

"Who's that, Slyv?" Malc asks on her laden return.

"Johnny Panic & The Lost Weekend, a rock band with my story name is playing. That's a compliment to me, don't you think? I was right when I said I'd never be rid of Johnny Panic, but I didn't mean in this way. This makes it a pleasant surprise. One I can live with, and the other part of their name, wasn't that a film, Malcolm? Oh sorry, sorry, I've just realised."

"Oh, it doesn't matter now, Sylv. Time has proven me right. My 'Under the Volcano' still sells every year, but nobody remembers that book, and at the time I was accused of tracing it. Me. Tracing! They were having a laugh, weren't they? Everyone today knows it as an old Ray Milland film, as you do. As I bet that band does."

They both smile.

"I wonder if they sing about me," she contemplates.

"Everyone does, doll. Everyone," the males reply.

CHAPTER TWENTY NINE

Late in the night, or early in the morning, the enlivened, enlivered Fulke decided to walk the West Hill route back into town, rather than walk around the common mentioned mound, to take in again the murder scene, somebody-seen, unrequited scene.

Returning to an unforgiving, fret threatened, hidden trove of evidence and avoidance not seen, as one does not seek one finds. He cannot find what he needs. He needs what he does not find.

Salter Lane slowly stepped up from the Old Town avoiding several large hedgehogs braving mankind and cooling themselves on the stone steps from the still, very warm night he affectionately smiled down on them. Reaching the top of these footsteps and about to cross the narrow Croft Road he avoided injury by quickly backstepping from an ageing, rusted automobile equipped with the ubiquitous, white, snow plough spoiler effect back and front, its young contender tunnel visioning ahead, speeding by, exhaust rattling, up the road to chance any of many oblivions known to man.

Climbing up the last lap of The Steepes, the West Hill slope, he trod and slipped on an animal scat but refused to fall, instead cursing his imbalance as he hopped one-legged randomly at first, then predictably bodily into the awaiting shrubs and bushes for facial and palm abrasions. The vegetation seemed to welcome him by enveloping his spoilt being, though he decided not to remain. Emerging fumed to silence he was placated noticing three young badgers at play further down the slope, feeling safe now the only energetic human awake had passed.

On nearing the Hill's peak he mumbled aloud into his authentically distressed leather coat collar, bibulous contrasting thoughts of the presented scene to yesterday's morbidity:

"Fast and low, mottled cloud form a pale, ruffled, complexion over the disturbed sea always attempting to invade the passive land like a shallow breathing lover before a rushed consummation. Thrifty fishing boat lights contrast the blackness of the vastness, while a farouche fret licks the East Hill slowly becoming its own transience."

"The last of the fucking romantics," he murmured to no-one. "I must write this down if there's still a market for it." Knowing he never would. Knowing there never would be.

As Fulke continued the slant of the mount to its geological summit, he noticed close ahead a male body popping up, silhouetting alternately in blind rhythm, signifying lust or love, passionately aroused beneath his salacious son of man on the brow of the knoll adjacent to where he knew the corpse was found. Behind the carefree couple the moon glistened on the sea which became an enormous gorilla's silverback and two fishing boats chugged out from shore, their V shaped wakes crossed to gradually part as the boats disappeared into slate shaded oblivion.

"That's ruined my flow. I can't use that! What time do they think it bloody is? There again this has to be the best time I guess. For them. Nobody around... Except a fucking, stupid copper who can't stop working, and they're getting hotter and hotter for each other by screwing where they shouldn't. I bet his brain's shrinking by the minute! The sodding signs we put up are still there, surely? Not even the kids could have taken them all down. Not in that short time. They'd just use 'em for goalposts anyway," he softly spoke inside before stopping.

The hill's height conquered with little breathlessness pride mixed with wonder informed him, he looked west beyond the permanently lit up cast iron, crustaceous, surgical instrument pinned pier onto Bexhill Bay up to the dark, occasionally diaphanous clouds, seemingly straightening the backs of the distant Downs defying low level aircraft as his body settled.

Walking to the crime spot his gaze narrowed to slowly roam over the haphazardly stacked, swerving streets of Hastings Newtown. The stepped, stunted and clasping buildings numbly knuckled to the slopes, gnawing and grasping skyward appearing to know not what they want, only let it be something, until his eyes settled on the working nightlights in a downtown block of flats.

The total luminescence forming a large cross which ran the whole length and height of the large sea-front building, witnessed from his distance coincidentally forming a symbol of international doctrinal recognition. Large and bright with a muted yellowish glow it would fool many a tribe in their folly. Some would see a sign and rejoice their faith, while others, he knew, would use this image to their selfish ends in gladness and providence and power, consuming the many sheepish comers without guilt.

He continued on the now mostly levelled ground, to the area where the recent impatient lovers consummated their curiosity and power before vacating, when the enveloping, directionless moonlight abruptly changed to a spotlight searing through cloud to speed his thoughts to notice the loose, fairy ring of mushrooms, a delicacy of a fungus braved by some and feared by the remainder, around where the youthful wantonness had triumphed.

"So they were hippies searching for a future, were they? What a funny way to find it!"

Comments of the sprightly couple he colourfully explored vividly echoing entrance and exit in mystic magical thoughts, but any of relevance?

Slowly.

Epiphany!

"There was a ring of chantrelles around the body but I didn't think anything of it!" He delighted to exclaim to the silence. "They grow often on the hill so I didn't take any notice of them, but... How can I be so sightless? Vanity! All is. The body was put in that particular place deliberately. The vanity of the murderer or murderers, and I couldn't see it."

Smiling, he moved back to the causeway to continue towards the domicile buildings off the grassland, only to touch, to bump into an old associate, drunk and happy.

John the Plane, so called because he survived a plane crash in which two hundred others died, was in a quandary and pleaded with Fulke for the use of his torch as it was desperately needed to find something that John the Plane had dropped. John let fall his blow on The Steepes coming up when he had started to roll a joint and he desperately needed Fulke's police torch to appease his sense of frustration. Acquiescing, Fulke and the worried survivor walked back down part of the slope with the torch more than doing its work, until at last John the Plane smiled. The plastic wrap around the drug reflected the narrow light to be gleefully retrieved with compliments all round as in an olympic win.

The chatting two recommenced the incline just as a silhouetted car began to drive down the pedestrian slope towards them.

In a hurry.

Full beamed lights scorching the darkness blaring sight to blindness like right wing regulators looking for niggers and yids and queers or popists and muslim fundamentalists, unbelievers in the darkness of a Hollywood adventure film.

The car speedily neared.

Fulke played the torch like his job. Confrontational. Melodramatic. Bright.

Pointed it straight at the fast, oncoming vehicle.

To both's surprise the car's gears made ugly, painful noises as it screeched to an unplanned, skidded halt. More crunching of metal, and the motor reversed at speed worthy of a hill climb, seemingly in the belief that the police were spot-checking moonlight toyboyjoy-riders.

By the time Fulke and John the Plane made the road there was silence in their world, and the vehicle seemed never to exist. Both nervously laughed at the episode.

After leaving John the Plane at the all night drinking club in town they visited next, Fulke, bored and sated now by company and booze, decided to walk home. Brushing Chekov's sculpture enough to cause a sway on entering the flat, he walked straight through to switch on the television, an early morning habit of his.

Kettle boiled he sat and drank black coffee. Wondering should he eat anything if there is anything, though he had no desire to prepare anything.

Three silverfish, *lepisma saccharina,* disturbed by his irresponsible, unsociable movements, waddled from under the sink unit to be lost again under curled up lino.

The television screen lamented the costs of a dying, capitalist society and indulged in advertising particular flesh.

Fulke pondered:
On late night tv. you can ring for a male
they advertise a gay way of living
imagine for a moment, only one, please prevail
the opposite number giving.
That is a man could ring for a woman
or to stretch things further
to sexual preferences inner
a woman could ring for a man.
Opposite partners
on loan for the evening
To return in the morning
No money back no guarantee
plays our new liberated society.

CHAPTER THIRTY

Mr. Rufus Rust is writing to the papers again.
The louche lines fall easily into place.
Sweat pellets hang to drizzle from his forehead as he relentlessly scribes;

Dear Newspaper Editor,
You insist on writing all this rabid nonsense about women dancing with men. Females do not have the same vitality of life, as they do not move the way men do. The traditional dances were created to suit the male physique. What are they trying to do? Would they accept women in rugby teams or football teams or cricket teams? No, they would not. It is tradition, don't they know? You do not alter tradition. No, you do not.

The women have their part to do, of course. Don't get me wrong, but...the future will be so different. Do you know that all churches are built on pagan sights, which is not to say of course that they are so, but...and ah...the future.

The traditional Mullah's Play which we act out shows the differences between good and evil. St. George is the good and, of course, the Turkish knight is the bad. St. George kills the bad one but the good doctor brings the knight back to life for a happy ending. Acceptable even for the young, and the future...no vehicles you see. Only bicycles. For men and women naturally. To be never again urban. Never again next door angst in a brave new world away from pollution and development where new truths can be seen all leading to the dance.

There will be no arguments, no political controversies, with everyone knowing their country and staying there. None of this EEC business, just a pursuit of green care and male jingling. The bicycle will take a fundamentalist position. Buzzing around on two wheels looking particularly impressive downhill. Ha ha! That trick reserved for the males of the species naturally.

Lastly, Morris dancing to be compulsory for boys in schools of all ages.

Your Obedient Dancer,
Rufus Rust The Bell'
King of the Robotic Mime and Morris Men.

He stopped to reform eco warrior thought and gazed beyond the tenebrous light of the big, white, rusty trailer open window out onto the already dazzling sun in its obvious hovering mid morning position committing its abundant apathy to spill over onto the plethora of pebbledashed mounds, open pools and coarse seakale, rubbery shrubbery cornered and curtailed by the hard edged, nuclear power station wall, and smelt the sea on the wind before recommencing his articulate, evangelical zeal.

There is life in gravel pit land.

Be it odd.

But then the phone rang as he was picking up his weights.

The police were feigning interest and substituting voices at play as Fulke needed to know R. Rust's exact whereabouts.

"Is that the Morris Men company?"

"Morris Men it is." R. Rust plays with one training weight.

"We need a dance group, you know, whatever you boys are called. We're arranging a festival of the elements."

"Speak up, I'm middle aged you know, but still a wonderful dancer."

"We could come and see you?"

"You could."

"Whereabouts are you then? What? Gravelpitville? Where's that then?"

"When you see Dungeness Power Station in your distance just follow the ley lines. That's why the power station was built where it was."

"Oh..er..right. See you in an hour to discuss it, yes?"

On the walk to D.I. Swettervil's car the two police officers talk and the bruised prisoner remains quiet. "There's just one reason why I don't like driving with the boss."

"Yes, I know."

"It's that damn noise he calls music. It goes on and on and on."

"I know. Don't remind me."

"What does he call it? Captain fucking Beefheart?"

The prisoner hears and speaks. "Captain Beefheart?"

"Yeah. Why?"

"It's brilliant."

"You mean you like it?"

"Of course, don't you?"

"No!" Both together.

"That's genius that is."

"Genius?"

"Genius! Definite!"

"Well, you know what you can do with that mush, mush!"

They were through Camber Sands and driving past the high, wire-fenced, Army Base taking fast, screeching corners while somewhere inside every traveller's mind along this stretch lodges the belief that the Army, by chance, could be using the firing ranges positioned just behind the wire as they drive by in their ignorance and fragility.

The landscape was gradually transforming from fertile foliage to shingleville, the sheep patterned landscape was turning to tender tundra and even Fulke noticed there were suddenly no trees for miles around.

The car passed by shingle beds interspersed with post quarried lakes where homing wind surfers slipped through the independent waters as on grease of their making. Single winged gossamers sailing the water up wind from that terrible life containing its seeping violence teasing into the persistent wind. The delicacies of this section of the nuclear reactor's surroundings default its presence there.

Unaware of how the long snaking road they drove down contrasted with the curt directness of the giant pylon lines bleeding radiated energy away to the hovels of the miserable and the mansions of the rich, they travelled by neglected cranes and mechanical belts having exercised function, loomed rust over gravel pits and damp dumps where primary coloured poppies created jealousies in the otherwise pasteled prettiness of plant life.

Two aged, stone lighthouses postured as sole sentinels each side of the three reactored, fifth decade, functionally designed power station.

A grey and dirty backdrop for old cheap adventure films, surrounded by extra thick pylons necessary to speed power away in a flat, failed alluvial landscape where workers learn about leaks from the television before the management.

Myths of varying ecological stances abound around the area, that revolve frantically into spins concerning this technology.

They begin with fish that are sucked into the turbines where they are chopped up and spat back into the food-chain which affects all sea food we consume; glowing in the dark packets of prawn cocktail crisps spotted by thieves raiding corner shops after dark, and end with Geiger counter carrying Greenpeace activists listening to the gravel while walking.

The unforgiving troupe persevered onwards past buildings of everything but brick, with a sceptic tank settled at each abode and invariably adjacent to large, colourful Rubbish Dumping Prohibited signs in an area that seemed to have been created for that sole purpose and revenue. Overturned rowing boats at the sides and half empty sacks of sand sitting singularly out the backs of corrugated huts called prefabricated buildings; money and home sweet home to the estate agents and home dwellers.

The many rabbits and few sheep fight for the sparse grasses of the grim landscape with the sometimes, scorch coloured, wild flowers for variation.

A row of identical, sea-front bungalows, each with the same politics, same patterned wallpaper, leaded windows and pampas grass gardens, lined the long thin coast road to the east, glowing with equal, small screen radiation seeing identical worlds inside and out, lost in old dreams and wasted time awaiting the occasional mercy killing, staring at these televisions late into the night to awake with new fears. Their spoilt youth in logoed, second-hand cars patrol their boredom, not knowing all they have to do is escape.

Above the moving men and machine and below a panorama of cirrus cloud, light planes flying right hand circuits at Lydd airport become confused by a squadron of low flying Canadian geese intermittently patrolling the runway. The flashing beacon of the airstrip's fire vehicle glimpsed through the dunes by the police and thief.

Driving towards this fantastic containment of energy and death, this pogrom of tangible limitations, the car eventually pulled off the road onto a shingle track between rotting gate posts. On the left decaying support was nailed a bordered board advertising a Greenpeace gig with Joe Stalin and the Whale Nukers, the ecology fucku band, playing a solace spree soon. The engine was cut, as ahead the uneven route was deemed impossible to negotiate further by the four sedentary travellers. They cursed communally and commenced walking.

Shoes crunching pebbles sounded no echo in Fulke's head. Seagulls, too, evoking no reverberating cries. *So this is how things sound without booze.*

"Wouldn't take long for those buggers to close down everything, would it?" D.C. Klens *recently promoted* indicated the energies aside.

"No I guess not," replied D.C. Nudge.

"Electricity workers, sewage workers and dustmen should be the most highly paid of the public sector," declared D.I. Swettervil.

"You mean as well as us?" said D.C. Klens.

"Well, no. More than us, I guess. We'd all be in the shit if they didn't work. Though I guess some would hardly notice. Some would probably revel in it."

The four walkers watched surfers out there playing with incoming waves as they trudged.

"Look! They're mainly sucking, tucking and ducking," D.C. Nudge points in their direction.

"What?"

"They don't turn, they rotate."

"Well I think they're reeling from toxic polymers," D.C. Klens shows off.

"Shit! So you do know?"

"I've done some."

"You and me both."

The boarders noticed them, came in and talked.

"So what are you lot doing here dressed like that?" a first surfer enquires.

Before they could claim their superiority another asked why they were there.

Another two water babies began arguing about how fast they moved over the surf, which quickly developed into whose board had the largest rocker.

The police had still not replied, being fixed in the barrage of bountiful language still rushing towards them. They continued listening to the rantings and gossip of these excited young ecological sea trimmers maintaining how wave heights have increased over the last few years, which is not supposed to happen on a stable planet.

It's freaky man. Like it's too worrying.

They find themselves agreeing with similar passion.

Listening on transfixed to a momentary muteness, they are assured of the fact that the surfers swimming near the nuclear power station will inevitably glow in old age if they make out that long. They continue to comment on how buildings were pure until people decayed them, though here it is probably the other way around, and they eventually answer the only question the police wanted to employ without the police asking the same when they mention where waves are highest, which had to be somewhere near a hippie's trailer as there is only the one in that area.

"Thanks, goodbye," the guardians of civilisation politely spoke.

The shoving around had stopped dead an awareness of their conservationalists stature in life. Watching them walk away one surfer enquired, "The one in the middle didn't look like a copper though, did he?"

The others threw him back into the sea.

Laughing

CHAPTER THIRTY ONE

"Cheerful out here, innit?" D.C. Klens said, staring at the lofty, imposing power station, giver of life and comfort but at such a cost. "Those warmly surfers fitted here, too, what?!"

"Plenty of colour, though. All over them," D.C. Nudge answered to score.

"Yeah. Just as well we're wearing shades," D.C. Klens without the grudge.

"Like real coppers, huh?"

"No, as humans caring for our eyes."

"Are we?" D.I. Swettervil knowing he was not, but now will.

Trudging.

Heavy and slowly through shingle.

"We've got something on him already," the D.I. spoke on the quiet.

"Yes, what's that?" D.C. Klens enquired, wondering why he had been told none of this before.

"There was something dubious about a possible arson attack on a laboratory so that the urine he gave after a breath test would not be found over the limit. And he diluted some more and paid to take it to a private laboratory where naturally it would be found clear," Swettervil continued, "and him a chuffing chemist!"

"He's a boy all right," D.C. Nudge answered, hopefully appropriate.

"We knew, but we couldn't catch him out."

"Bless him!"

Their prisoner says nothing, merely follows behind the group, obedient in defeat. Fulke believes taking J. Small along will speed things up.

Or the opposite.

Or cause a chaos.

They soon reach the decaying metal caravan, mount its creaky steps and enter the inside without knocking.

A flicker in Rufus Rust's eye receiving four people, denotes he recognises the prisoner but his immediate, gleaming smile acts out his defence. "Er..hello. Can I help you at all? What is this, Swettervil, old man? Are you here about the dance gig?"

The accompanying lawmen, seeing a short, muscular pugilist of a man, realise it would be better to talk this situation through. They need not have worried, as D.I. Swettervil naturally had a plan, being aware of R. Rust's physique.

"You could say that! We've come to arrest you for robbery. Of town coffers...my town's coffers...oh...and murder... That's all old ... old boy," slowly smiles the face of the detective inspector while implying to the three listeners that harming his town is a far greater crime than mere murder.

"You can't prove it! Just because he says so!" R. Rust points to the prisoner, knowing as he does so he has lost the plea of ignorance. He attempts a reversal of the impossible and acts out a tangent. "Where are my manners? Let me show you out."

The thin, metal walls of the small, contained living quarters begin to seep, strain and build up with the power of potential violence.

D.I. Swettervil, browsing again on the morris dancer's muscled form, does not think the police would win an all out embrace of brutality quickly, and demands his mind to deliver alternatives.

"We told him you'd deny it and he didn't seem too pleased. That's why we brought him along." The Detective Inspector sounds chirpy, incidental and matter of fact.

"I don't know this person, Swettervil, I tell you. I don't," in a tone that implies all have forgotten what he spoke earlier.

"You will intimately, and very soon if you don't say what we want to hear," D.C. Nudge chips in, not seeing why he cannot be part of the pack.

"This is coercion."

"Is it?" D.C. Nudge likes these bits.

"I'll take the cuffs off him and we'll see what he'll do, should I?" D.I. Swettervil asks as he does so.

"That's against the law."

"Yes it is, isn't it?" D.C. Nudge butting in again to his dominating D.I.'s annoyance.

"Why you...!" Violence like a faithful lover's promise commences bellowing forth when R. Rust reaches across the narrow shell of an interior to strike the recently handcuffed.

Before he can touch the released player, the liberated prisoner interjects with the strength of inequality born in retribution and slams the metal of his cuffs in the vanquishing angle hard into R. Rust's mouth of gold fillings. R. Rust gasps and falters a few seconds, astonished by this focused fatwah, coughing and spluttering a grainy spray of dull yellow, precious metal along with sharp spurts of healthy, dark red blood over his assailant. His head instantly becoming a psychedelic wrap of aches and colours. Enough time to allow the law to perform their act of curtailment and add similar, shiny adornments to his strong tanned, hairy wrists.

"All right. I ... I admit it." Seeing himself confined.

"That's better," D.C. Klens speaks knowing he could no longer cramp his D.I.'s style. His confidence lifts as he begins to practice his college economics. "The taxpayer will now look after you. For a very long time."

R. Rust, surprisingly meek now, is taken away by the confident duo.

Plus one.

The one he should watch.

Last out, D.I.. Fulke Swettervil is about to leave the neglected trailer, when he notices books that had fallen off R. Rust's walnut desk in the slight struggle. He bends down to pick them up, noticing their titles. The first perceived and catalogued is a book of safe eating mushrooms that he immediately drops again when he sees...

'The Hammer, The Sickle and The English Rose': New venturing poems by Xaviera Hume.

In suspended astonishment he turns the book over now more curious to see where R. Rust's bookmark rests.

He looks aghast at the poem's prosaic heading.

'Byron and Shelley
My brothers in the struggle'
He reads on..

We follow your youthful stare
aged I still cannot compete,
You were dead
before the realisation in others lives sprung
solemnly prolific
while we had not begun
to breathe the same chaste air.
Vanity pass me by
life short and sweet
with a new meaning to deep heat
we merely cry;
while a sister's tale ringing still loud
primogenitorially malproud.

He looks up in the direction of the sea and violently throws the book out the creaking door towards its salty fate, not knowing the tide will bring the pages quickly back inland. Closing the trailer entrance quietly behind, he commences the return shingle shank to the car. As he does, so an opened letter falls from his pocket. D.I. Swettervil unaware hurries to catch up to his work-mates. The wind notices only the objects it carries and controls as the dispatch rises only to sink and settle in a sheltered scoop of sand, where any curious bystander can retrieve and glance on the knowledge printed there which proclaims...

> Flickerkindle (International) plc
> 666 Ocean Esplanade
> Folkestone
> X6 YZ999
>
> Dear Friend,
> The offer of a directorship with our world renowned gas central heating firm still holds though I have written to you twice before offering the same. How well you treat me in the police force can never be satisfactorily repaid. After all, you saved my life more than once, Fulke. I cannot forget that. Accordingly my repeated offer still remains against all other considerations. I really want you to join us.
> Please reply indicating whether you wish to be part of our successful enterprise or not.
> Remember the door will always be open.
> Yours sincerely,
>
> Ex Detective Constable Eric Filey,
> St Leonard's C.I.D., Currently Acting Managing Director.

Shoes crunching shingle Fulke closes on his associates in crime and their prisoner, watching their prisoner, all consecutively passing a fenced, light brown, New Forest Pony chewing the limited grasses. As he walks he ponders whether to bring up the subject of an alternative lifestyle with Bo tonight as they drink down the Old Town, or perhaps look around the heating business offer secretly before committing himself or the both to anything new.

After all, she might start choosing flowery, embossed wallpapers and a peach bathroom suite and garish, hippie duvet covers and a blue tiled kitchen and a racing green fridge freezer and a tasteful dishwasher, and continental cast iron saucepans and an ultramarine wood burning stove and a P.C. for their accounts, and an electric tin opener and partial solar heating and a Spanish style padded, purple PVC corner bar with a football ice bucket, and a water bed and a house name plate and a satellite dish and his and hers bath towels and robes, and Wilton carpets all through the expensive, sea-front house with a new, massive, Japanese four-by-four people carrier and personalised number plate in the security lit garage, and pampas grasses and yucca plants for the front garden and bright, primary coloured gnomes around the netted, carp pond out the veranda back. And start again discussing the positive dynamics of a large family.

And...And...And...And...Jesus! What's happening?

He could feel himself being drawn to some of this! No! No! Not that far! Go and see first!

As he trudges he searches pockets for the missing letter.